TO THE BIGHORNS

BUCKSKIN CHRONICLES BOOK 4

B.N. RUNDELL

D1114647

WOLFPACK
PUBLISHING
— EST 2013 —

To The Bighorns is a work of fiction. Any references to historical events, real people or real places are used fictitiously. Other names, characters, places and events are products of the author's imagination, and any resemblance to actual events, places or persons, living or dead, is entirely coincidental.

Published in the United States by Wolfpack Publishing

Wolfpack Publishing
6032 Wheat Penny Avenue
Las Vegas, NV 89122

wolfpackpublishing.com

Library of Congress Control Number: 2018951317

Paperback ISBN: 978-1-62918-635-1
eBook ISBN: 978-1-62918-666-5

This is dedicated to the love of my life, without her this and any other work ever accomplished by me would not have been possible. Her support, inspiration, and encouragement gives meaning to each and every day and purpose to my life. My wife, Dawn, has faithfully been by my side for over a half-century and she's planning on that much more. So, thank you, my beloved. And to my children and grandchildren who have repeatedly expressed their pride in this old man and have continually been a source of pride for me and mine.

TO THE BIGHORNS

THE BRILLIANT GOLD OF THE EMERGING SUN that forced its way between the horizon and the clouds seemed to stretch its arms across the horizon and paint the trackless snow with a muted, reflected glow.

Jeremiah stood with one ankle crossed over the other and leaning against the scratchy bark of the massive Douglas fir that stood as a sentinel at the edge of the black timber climbing the mountain behind him. Looking between the towering peaks of the Absaroka Range, he reveled in the familiar scene before him. This was his time of the day and a time of solitude he enjoyed while he communed with his God. A thankful man, Jeremiah spent such times reflecting on his life and the many blessings he enjoyed. His family had grown much faster than he ever expected.

First when he promised his dying sister that he would take her son and raise him as his own, then the addition of Clancy Mae, the redhead waif and sole survivor of the massacred wagon train and, of course, the newest addition, the son presented him by his beloved wife, Laughing Waters. That son, Little John, was only little in size as he was certainly a handful at just over two-years-old.

It seemed that sometimes it took all the rest of the family just to keep track of that little one as he scampered about on his short stubby legs and little beaded moccasins. Yet, even though he was little, his giggles and smiles brought joy to everyone he encountered and Jeremiah never knew before how much joy and pride a child could bring to a family.

This was the end of the second winter the village of Black Kettle's Arapaho spent in this high mountain valley of the Absaroka. Spring was starting to show itself in the many anticipated ways seen only in the mountains of the Rockies. Aspen were budding out and would soon burst forth with their new green quaking leaves. Pines now lifted previously snow-burdened limbs skyward and bent towards the sun. Green shoots of the meadow grasses were littered with sprigs of spring flowers that stretched heavenward to soon share blossoms of color. Snowdrifts at the top edge of the granite peaks were dwindling and sharing their moisture to fill the thirsty streams that lifted a chorus of gurgling waterfalls. As the line of golden sunlight slowly dropped with the rising sun, the valley awakened with the sounds of a busy village. Jeremiah basked for another moment as the sun warmed his buckskins then moved to return to his cabin and his family.

Pulling the latchstring and pushing the door open, Jeremiah stepped into the warmth of the cabin that housed memories as well as family and friends. Scratch was standing by the fireplace with outstretched hands and glazed over eyes as he contemplated the coming day. The grizzled mountain man appeared to be twice his age with his bent back and bow-legged stance. With a head surrounded by hair and whiskers that fought one another for some semblance of direction, his red bob nose and sparkling eyes revealed a man less than a decade older than Jeremiah.

The two had been friends several years and had shared many adventures. Jeremiah, known as White Wolf among the Arapaho, watched Jeremiah's wife as she busily prepared their morning meal. With fingers working through dough and a touch of flour on her cheek, her beauty still stirred Jeremiah with thoughts of appreciation and love. The two had grown to maturity together in the Arapaho village as Jeremiah, the adopted son of the escaped slave Ezekiel, and Laughing Waters were often in competition with one another in the many games and exercises practiced by the young people of the village. Often joining the two was Broken Shield, the half-brother of Waters and Jeremiah's best friend. Waters had proven to be the better marksman with a bow and arrow, but Jeremiah was better with a rifle. All three were excellent hunters and Waters had even bested most of the warriors in the village and earned the respect of all. The daughter of the Shaman and leader of the tribe, she was readily accepted as a warrior and healer.

"Owww!" came an outburst from the loft and the rising Caleb. "That danged timber will do me in yet," he grumbled as he crawled to the edge and the ladder, "but I'm about ready to carve out a space for my head before I wake up dead one morning!" He stepped down the ladder as he was talking, though no one was paying much attention to his normal morning banter.

He joined the two men by the fireplace and Waters noticed that from behind, the three looked like stair-steps with Jeremiah barely taller than their son, Caleb, who was also known as Talks to the Wind. Both men were broad of shoulder, thick of chest, and had tapered torsos to muscular legs that spoke of the many miles they had traveled together. Scratch was solidly built, just a bit shorter than Caleb, but equally as broad and muscled. The three men presented a trio of proven warrior mountain men and as the saying goes, 'would do' to ride the river with.

As the rough-hewn door pushed open, all turned to see Clancy Mae struggling with a wooden bucket of splashing water. The slender girl had a tangle of curly red hair framing a freckled face and flashing green eyes. Her look of consternation spoke before her words were expelled, "Well, you lazy bunch of so-called men, come help a lady willya?" Setting down the bucket in the doorway, she leaned against the doorframe and was silhouetted by the rising sun. *She really is the Sun of the Morning just as Black Kettle named her,* thought Caleb as he stepped toward the girl to give his able-bodied assistance. They smiled at one another as they shared thoughts and memories of their many adventures together.

Since she joined this family over two years ago, she had rapidly won the hearts of everyone and had grown in the ways of the mountains with skills in hunting, tracking and warrior-in-training feats that rivaled others her own age. Caleb and Clancy were inseparable and seldom acted independently in any activity or task. Both young people had excelled in learning everything their parents, Scratch, or members of the village sought to teach them. Together they had grown into respected members of the village and were often chosen for special responsibilities and missions.

"All right everyone, get to the table or at least get out of my way so I can finish this meal," ordered Waters. "Clancy Mae, check those biscuits and set 'em on the table. I'll finish the rest."

The shuffling of feet and the scraping of the chairs on the hard packed dirt floor signaled the willing and hungry men were obeying their instructions. Tin plates and cups clattered as each setting was placed in front of the men and at the empty places for the ladies. Scratch poured his coffee, then Jeremiah's and handed the coffee pot across the table to Caleb. "So, whatcha got on yore mind for us to be doin' taday?" asked Scratch as he looked to the head of the table and Jeremiah.

"I'm kinda anxious to get some fresh meat. Now that the snow's cleared off a mite, I figure the elk might be comin' up higher or maybe some bear might be comin' outta their winter quarters. Either or suits me, long as it ain't dried, smoked or jerked. Wouldn't you like to sink your teeth into some fresh liver or at least a nice juicy steak?" asked Jeremiah.

"Uhhh yeah, now thatcha mention it, believe I would. Course, I ain't complainin' mind you. Cuz Water's cookin' caint be beat, but a nice bloody steak would shore hit the spot." ·

With eyes squinting and an eyebrow raised, Waters said, "You better not complain, you old warbag you. Don't you think this woman would like a fresh slice of elk liver too?"

Shaking her head and shrugging her shoulders, Clancy Mae piped in with, "Ewww, ya'll can have my share. I don't cotton to eatin' guts of any kind. Now, a steak would be O.K. but you can have all the guts. No thank you."

As the ladies seated themselves, Jeremiah said, "Before we get too carried away with meat we don't have, let's give thanks for the meal before us," and bowed his head and began his short prayer of thanksgiving. As he concluded with "Amen", the rest echoed his closing and the meal was shared around the table.

Waters smiled as she thought how thrilled she was with this, every day event and how she never tired of having her family together at the table. She held Little John on her lap and hugged him close while he reached for another corn meal biscuit on her plate. The tow-headed boy was her pride and joy, though she loved each of her adopted children equally, it was the total dependency of the baby that brought out new emotions and wonder she had never experienced. She was still amazed at the blonde hair although Jeremiah explained that he and his sister were both tow heads until their teen years when their darker brown color predominated. She simply saw it as a gift from the Great Spirit and reveled in the special nature of her young son.

The chatter around the table stopped and the momentary silence brought Waters from her reverie.

Noticing that everyone was looking at her, she asked, "What?"

Jeremiah responded, "We were asking what you women-folk had planned for the day. I thought we," indicating the three men, "would head down to that lower valley and do some hunting and get some fresh meat. Have you got something that you and Clancy were planning on doing?"

With a wink at her daughter, Waters replied, "Don't you know we always have something planned. If we left everything up to you men, we'd not only go hungry, we'd probably freeze to death as well."

"Hummph, well if that's the way you feel about it, I guess we better go 'bout provin' you wrong, as usual," snidely commented Jeremiah. "Course, some things we don't necessarily have to go provin', they just is, that's all. So, you women just take care of your sewin', stitchin', and whatever else you're gonna be doin' and us men'll take care of the important things, like huntin' and such." Smiling, he nodded to Scratch and Caleb and they rose from the table to prepare for the day's hunt.

After the men departed, Waters told Clancy to get their horses and they would get started as well. "You mean; we're going hunting too?" asked the girl with a smile painting her face.

"If we don't, we probably won't have that fresh meat the men were talking about," she said with a bit of a giggle. "They're good at talking, but when there's that many together, they can't shut up and the game usually stands behind the trees and laugh at them. You rig the horses and I think I'll have Pine Leaf join us." Pine Leaf was the wife of Broken Shield and a leader of the Crow Nation. Although she and Shield lived with the Arapaho, she maintained contact with the Crow village that rested on the Eastern side of the Absaroka Mountain Range.

Clancy led the two horses to the steps of the cabin, tied them off and finished saddling both mounts. Her mind returned to the time when her family and the small wagon train was attacked by Crow warriors and the rest of the wagon train was massacred by the warriors led by Pine Leaf. Clancy had watched from the nearby bushes as her mother was killed by a lance thrown by this fearsome war leader of the Crow. Although that was over two years past, the image was fresh in Clancy's mind. The two had talked about that day and Pine Leaf explained that the whites were enemies of the Crow and though she led the attack, she would not have killed her mother except Clancy's mum had killed two of her warriors and Pine Leaf acted in defense of her men. The explanation was the closest thing to an apology that Pine Leaf had ever given and she continued to win the friendship of Clancy since she lived with the Arapaho and the people of Clancy's adopted mother, Laughing Waters.

Leaf and Waters soon joined Sun of the Morning, Clancy's Arapaho name, with Little John attired in his red and black wool capote and she carried an additional blanket if needed. Waters mounted and Clancy handed Little John to his mother then climbed aboard her blue roan to follow Waters and Pine Leaf making their way through the timber. Clancy knew her adopted mother was an excellent hunter and she was excited about another hunt with this respected warrior of the village.

Clancy had learned much from her mother and had grown in her skill with the bow to rival even Waters with her marksmanship. Still, learning the skills of tracking and understanding wild game, Clancy had proven to be a willing student of the wild. Now with two proven warriors and hunters to learn from, she intended to hone her skills and become like them.

THE EDUCATION OF Caleb was an ongoing process, from reading the scriptures every night to the vast catalog of knowledge gained on a wilderness expedition. The men he traveled with were willing participants in this process and reveled at every opportunity to impart the bits and pieces of their knowledge of animals, other Native tribes, and the wilderness. Shield was the most adept at identifying the many plants that were of use for medicines or to consume and Jeremiah and Scratch teamed up to share their wisdom regarding the behavior of the many animals and birds found in these Rocky Mountains.

But it was more than just the accumulation of knowledge concerning things and animals, but wisdom regarding relationship with other peoples and other individuals. The interaction between the many native peoples, many of whom considered themselves enemies, and others that were more peaceful and the differing beliefs of the different groups was an area of learning that Caleb sought mostly from Broken Shield.

Now as they followed the trail that led down to the lower valley, it was common for any of the men to point out an object, a sign, a track or an animal and expect Caleb to identify and elaborate on the subject. Jeremiah caught the boy's attention and pointed to the right of the trail. When Caleb neared that point, he looked and identified, "That's bear scat, from here it looks to be about a day old and from a Grizzly. Those tracks say he's movin' slow, probably just outta his den and hungry." Receiving a nod of approval from his Pa he looked overhead and watched a circling red tailed hawk. He let loose with a "keeeeeer" that caught the attention of the hawk and caused the bird to swoop a little lower to identify this ground bound hawk. Caleb had earned the name He Who Talks to The Wind from Black Kettle, the leader of the Arapaho village and his adopted grandfather, because he had a natural ability to mimic just about any sound made by the birds and animals that dwelt in these mountains. His gift was such that almost no one could distinguish the difference between the original and the mimic.

Scratch shook his head as he often did when he heard the boy's hawk cry. It had been a surprise to him when he realized the boy's ability to so correctly mimic the calls of practically every bird and animal known. *Sometimes I think that boy can actually talk to them animals,* thought the mountain man. Scratch noticed a track near the trail and clucked his tongue to get the boy's attention and pointed at the track. When Caleb neared the spot, he leaned from his mount to get a closer look and straightened up to answer his Uncle Scratch, "That there's a mountain lion and fresh too. Course y'all from the flatlands call 'em catamounts or panthers or pumas. It looks like he's limpin' a little, that left front paw might be injured. That would make 'em a mite more dangerous, wouldn't it?"

"That's right, squirt! Usually a painter wouldn't be a threat to man, but when one of 'ems wounded or hurt somehow, they'll take any game of opportunity. Specially, if they cain't run so good. That's good seein' boy, most folks woulda missed that."

The hunters split up with Jeremiah and Shield taking the south edge of the valley while Scratch and Caleb hung near the edge of the timber on the North edge. With a full moon the night before, most high altitude animals, elk, deer, big horn sheep and others would feed during the light of the moon when danger would be less with the diminished sight. Then, when full daylight came the animals would wander back into the thick timber and find a bed to sleep off the night's binge during the heat of the day. Most of the animals still wore their winter coats and with the coming of warmer weather, the hot sun of the afternoon was a good excuse for a nap. The hunters moved along the edge of the timber watching for tracks of animals that had moved from the river or the coming-green grass of the meadow into the timber. But apart from a rare set of tracks made by a single animal that had returned from a night's drink, there was no sign of even a small herd of elk that would tempt the hunters. After riding almost three miles along the timber, they decided to meet by the river and fix a pot of coffee and do some damage to the jerky they carried.

Jeremiah and Shield had the fire started and the coffee going when Scratch and Caleb joined the men for their late morning break. Dropping from their mounts, they loosened the cinches and tethered the horses near those of Jeremiah and Shield.

"So, that there Java 'bout ready? This ol' boy is sorely in need of some o' that black tar," stated Scratch as he winked at Caleb. "This hyar huntin' fer them elusive wapiti is hard work, ain't it boy?"

"Is that what we're doin'? I thought we was just gittin' away from the women for a while," replied Caleb.

"Whatchu mean, gittin' away from the women? What women you tryin' to get away from?" asked Jeremiah with a grin.

"Ah, you know. All of 'em I guess," murmured Caleb.

"When you get older, you won't be so anxious to get away from them," kidded Shield.

"Ahh, they're all confusin', I don't know what I'm s'posed to be feelin' anyhow," said Caleb. The men looked from one to another with grins tugging at their faces. All of them had noticed the way Caleb and Clancy had been almost inseparable for the last year, and such thoughts brought back memories of their own teen years and the thoughts between boys and girls.

"What do you mean confusing?" asked Jeremiah soberly.

"Well, you know. All you guys, like Scratch there. He and Charlie, or Charlotte, seemed to fit together real well, liked the same things and all and couldn't stay away from each other so they up and got hitched and now he's single again. And you, Shield, your wife tried to kill you first and she acted like she hated you and wanted to cut your liver out and the next thing we know, you was marryin' her. An' you Pa. You told me how you and Ma was always arguin' and fightin' before you got hitched and you even ran off to Kentucky an all, then brought me out here and all of a sudden, you was trottin' off to the marriage teepee. It's confusin' I tell ya!"

"Ya know, the boy's got a point there, Jeremiah, he shore does. Wimmin is confusin' varmints they is," stated Scratch. Shield chuckled in agreement and Jeremiah said in a low growl to Scratch, "You ain't no help." Then turning to Caleb he asked, "Son, it's not your place to figure out everybody else and their problems. What happens to others won't necessarily happen to you."

"Yeah but, how's a man supposed to know what to do if he can't learn from those around him?"

"Does this have something to do with Clancy?"

Caleb looked sharply at his Pa as if he let the cat out of the bag and mumbled, "Yeah, I guess so. One time I can't stand not being with her and the next I can't stand being around her. I don't know what's goin' on in my mind. How's a fella sposed to know when it's the right woman anyhow?" he asked looking around the circle of three men.

"Don't ask me. I thought I knew, but I found out I could read bear sign easier than I could understand wimmin," stated Scratch as he threw up his arms in disgust.

"How'd you know Pa? How'd you know you wanted to be hitched up with Waters?"

"Well," he muttered, "I think I always felt that way, but for a while I was unsure. But when it came time for me and Scratch to go downriver and Waters had to bring Shield here back to the village, that parting kinda stuck in my craw and I didn't want to be away from her. Come to find out she felt the same way and made me promise to come back to her, and I'm glad I did."

"Yeah, don't you 'member how miserable he'd get when we was travelin' with that wagon train and he'd get to mumblin' to himself. He was thinkin' 'bout Waters and wantin' ta' git back here to her," reminded Scratch.

"So, you're sayin' maybe if it came to leavin' I'd get a clearer picture of what I'm feelin'?"

"No, son, it's not that at all. It's different with everyone and it's just something you're gonna have to work out on your own. But, I'm sure that when the time comes, you'll know it. But I think you've got plenty of time before you have to make that decision."

"I hope so," answered Caleb. *But at times, I'm not even sure what I want to do with the rest of my life. I don't know if I'm supposed to be with Clancy and I love the mountains and my family and friends, but sometimes I get to thinkin' about the way things were back before my real ma died and I joined up with Jeremiah. I don't think I want to go back to the city way of livin' but what am I to do? Just become more Indian than white man, or become a mountain man and do what? Hmmm . . .* thought the boy.

Waters had yielded the lead to Pine Leaf and she and Clancy now followed her through the black timber. They were headed to the upper end of the smaller valley that rested on a shoulder of the towering Absaroka Mountains. Waters was certain they would find some elk that had followed the green-up of early spring into the higher elevations. Elk would usually drop to the lower elevations where there was less snow during the winter and graze was easier to find, but as soon as green-up came, most would make their way to the higher elevations and the cooler temperatures that were more comfortable with their winter coats.

She was counting on some early arrivals to the high meadow and she soon found her intuition was correct. As they approached the edge of the timber, Leaf motioned for them to stop and drop from their mounts. As they stealthily walked forward, Waters swung Little John into a blanket wrap that nestled him on her back. The three hunters huddled behind a cluster of kinnikinnick and plotted their hunt. Five elk were lazily grazing across the fresh green sprigs that dotted the meadow before them, facing away from the hunters. Soon the hunters started their stalk and split off to assigned places.

The plan was for Leaf and Clancy to work around the small herd to the upper fringe of the valley, launch their attack which would probably drive the animals back in the direction of Waters where she would get a chance at her kill. Within about fifteen minutes, the two stalkers arrived at the edge of the timber and entered the tall grass on all fours. Waters had made her way to a cluster of boulders and brush that protruded a short distance into the meadow and she now awaited the move of her fellow hunters. Leaf whispered to Clancy, "Move off to your right about five or six paces, and signal me when you're ready. I'll let you take the first shot, and I'll make mine when they move."

Short moments later, Clancy turned back to Leaf and nodded her head. She had spotted a sizable cow that appeared to be nice and fat and not with calf, probably a big yearling that she chose for her target. At the nod of Leaf's head, Clancy slowly rose to one knee with just the top of her bow and her shock of red hair above the grass, already at full draw, she let the arrow fly to its target. The whisper of death was a silent killer as the arrow buried itself deep in the lower chest just behind the front leg. The elk raised its head, started to trot off but within just five steps it halted, took one more hesitant step, and fell over. Before Clancy's target had taken two steps, Leaf let fly her arrow that likewise found its mark in a young bull that had just sprouted a short stub of antler. It too was only able to take a few steps before falling. The other animals quickly scattered in different directions and in their panic, sought protection in the higher reaches of black timber and did not approach the perch of Laughing Waters.

Clancy jumped to her feet and seeing the animals gone, she shouted to Waters, "Hey Ma! I got one! My first one with a bow!"

Leaf laughed at her and said, "That was a fine shot too. You are becoming a very good hunter and marks-man." Clancy looked at the older woman and smiled, beaming at the compliment from this proven warrior and leader.

The dressing out and de-boning of the animals was quickly accomplished with the skilled hands of the experienced women. All the while the three women talked, both instructing and sharing with Clancy, enjoying the special time together. As they bundled the meat in the hides to pack on the horses, Clancy asked the women, "How do you know when you find the right man for your husband?"

With shocked expressions on their faces, the women looked at each other, then at Clancy. Waters asked, "What is there about blood and guts that made you think about a man for a husband?"

Laughing, Clancy said, "It wasn't the blood and guts, it's just doin' things together, you know, like husband and wife. Both of you seem to be real happy with your husbands and I want that too, but how do you know ya got the right one?"

Waters smiled and thought about the last two years and how Clancy and Caleb had grown so much together and how they reminded her of the times she and Jeremiah had spent together. Thinking about those good times brought a smile to her face as she answered, "Are you thinking about Caleb?"

Clancy dropped her head, but her blush was evident before she moved. Even with her red hair covering her face, Waters knew she hit a tender spot in the girl's emotions. She answered, "Yeah, I suppose. Not like there's very many others to be thinkin' 'bout."

Leaf interjected, "Sometimes it grows on you and you

just know you can't live without them, kind of like Waters and White Wolf. But other times, it just comes on you by surprise, like it was with me and Broken Shield. I had no thoughts about taking a mate and hadn't even considered it, until I met Shield. It scared me at first, but it didn't take long before I knew that we were supposed to be together and I couldn't imagine life without him."

"She's right, it's different with everyone. Maybe you and Caleb are to be together and that would make me very happy. But it might be that the Great Spirit will bring you someone else like He did with Leaf and that would also make me very happy. I think you'll just have to wait and give it time. You are still young and have lots of time," consoled Waters.

"Yeah, maybe, but I knew a lot of girls my age that were already gettin' married."

The two women gave Clancy reassuring smiles, packed up the elk bounty on the horses, mounted up, and headed home with ample fresh meat for both families.

The disappointed hunters from the lower valley arrived at the village with long faces knowing the women would probably deride them mercilessly about their failures. Little did they know the women mounted their own hunting expedition and were returning at the same time from the upper reaches of the village. Caleb was the first to spot the small caravan of women and announced to the men, "Uh, fellas, I think we are in trouble," as he motioned with his chin at the returning successful hunters.

It was obvious that all three horses were loaded with extra bundles behind the riders and it took little guesswork to conclude what the elk-skin packs held. The broad grins on the faces of the women betrayed the bold confidence of the hunters and their planned attack on the manhood of each of the normally braggartly bunch of men. However, the women kept silent but said all that needed to be said with body language. As the two groups met, Waters slipped from her bounty laden horse still carrying Little John in the blanket pack on her back. She motioned to the men and grunted like a disgruntled brave, "Hunters return with meat. You squaws fix."

And with that the other two women dismounted, pulled the packs from their horses, and followed Waters to her cabin. As they entered the dwelling, giggles could be heard by each of the men that were now looking at the retreating backs of the successful hunters. With glances at one another, Jeremiah finally stated what all knew to be true, "I don't think we're gonna hear the end of this."

MID-MORNING IN THE HIGH COUNTRY VALLEY revealed the coming green of the aspen groves that stretched their probing fingers into the black of the pine forest. Under the bold sun of spring in the Rockies, the green valley was coming alive with sprigs of grass and the buds and blooms of flowers. *It's a good day to be alive,* thought Jeremiah as he strolled through the village en route to the buffalo hide lodge of Broken Shield.

With the coming of spring and the members of the village anticipating a move to summer grounds, Jeremiah had given considerable thought about the recent conversation with Caleb. He knew how the boy was feeling and he wanted to help but was at loss as to what would be best. But for now, he planned to surprise the boy with a special birthday. Arriving at Shield's lodge, he scratched the hide by the flap to seek entrance. A warm greeting bid him wait, and soon Shield came out of his dwelling bearing the tools and makings for fashioning arrows. With a nod he bid Jeremiah to be seated on a buffalo robe spread near the teepee and the two men leaned on the backrests made of peeled willow branches. "What brings my brother to my lodge this morning?" asked Shield.

"Are you and Leaf plannin' on visitin' her folks o'er at the Crow village before we go to our summer grounds?" asked Jeremiah.

"Yes. We will make a short visit there and return to move the village."

"Well, I got a little favor to ask . . . " began Jeremiah. After explaining to his friend what he was planning and receiving an enthusiastic response, Jeremiah rose to return to his cabin and continue his preparations for his big surprise. As he walked through the village, he spotted Caleb approaching and paused to speak with the boy.

"Whatcha up to today, son?"

"I'm goin' to see grandfather Black Kettle. He has some more medicine man stuff he wants me to know and he's helpin' me make a new bow and some new arrows, too," answered Caleb enthusiastically. "He's also got some flint and he promised to show me a bit about flint knapping."

"Sounds like you've got quite a day ahead of you. All right then, I'll see you this evenin' 'bout supper time." Father and son parted ways with each bearing his own secrets. Jeremiah knew the ways of Black Kettle and although the boy was doing most of the work, both the knowledge and the weapons were to be presents to the young man. And he also knew that Caleb was crafting some of the arrows as a gift for Clancy. The birthdays of both youngsters were just over a week apart and the family usually celebrated them together. Birthdays were of less importance to the Arapaho than the traditional celebrations observed by white men, but they were honored nevertheless.

Lifting the latch string and pushing in the door, he was greeted with squeals from the two women seated at the table. Clancy jumped up and snatched something from the table and held it behind her back. Looking at the two women with scowls on their faces, Jeremiah said, "What's wrong with you two? You'd think I was a Black-foot warrior on a raid or somethin' the way you're carryin' on."

"We thought you might be Caleb. Clancy is workin' on a new tunic for him for his birthday and she didn't want him to see it," answered Waters as Clancy returned to her seat and lay the tunic on the table. It was a soft tanned buckskin with fringed sleeves and she was working on the decorations of beads and porcupine quills. From what Jeremiah could see, it was going to be an exceptional garment.

"Well, there's just a little over a week before the big day rolls around. But it's lookin' mighty good. I'm sure you'll finish in time," he encouraged with a smile. He went to a tall narrow cabinet near the back door and rummaged around picking out some items, then gathering them together he walked out the back door without saying anymore to the busy ladies at the table.

"Greetings, grandfather," said Caleb as he approached the older man seated by the entrance to his hide lodge. Receiving a smile of welcome and a wave to a seat from the grey-headed medicine man, Caleb dropped beside his grandfather and noticed a large flat stone sitting in front of the crossed legs of the man. Without any wasted motion or words, the tutor began, "We will start today working with flint. This stone has been used by my people for many generations and has been a most important tool with many uses. First, we'll start with the blade for an axe."

He then began to show by example the art of flint knapping, an art that sometimes required striking with a stone but more often the slow applying of pressure to carefully break off small bits from the area of flint in order to shape it into a sharp edge for the tool. After considerable trial and error on the part of the student, Caleb finally began to understand the intricacies of the skill and successfully fashioned his first, crude arrow-head. With that accomplished, Black Kettle continued his instruction in the many other skills he sought. They spent time with the selection of willow for the shafts of arrows, the curing and shaping of those shafts, and the splitting of the ends for the insertion of the arrowheads that required the wrapping of the split and the inserted flint with thin strips of rawhide. With special dexterity, he learned to apply the glue on the edge of the split eagle feathers to apply the fletching to the arrows that would guide their flight.

For the remainder of that week, Caleb spent every day with Grandfather learning new skills and improving each skill to the level of competence necessary to fashion the chosen tools and weapons. The ability to identify the many plants was an ongoing education but he was thrilled to learn about such plants as the Nettle Leafed Horsemint, the leaves used for tea and a mild sedative, or the inner bark of the chokecherry that could be made into a tea for headaches and coughs, and so it went with each day bringing new discoveries, knowledge, and skills.

This was the kind of education that interested Caleb much more than just reading as his father had emphasized, although he knew all learning would be beneficial.

"Hey, ya gonna sleep all day, birthday boy? How 'bout you, birthday girl?" came the cry from below the loft and reaching up to smack the ears of the sleeping youngsters. The usual routine was a bump from below on the boards that made up the floor of the loft and the resulting thump, thump would awaken the sleeping pair. However, this crude and shocking alarm caused them both to sit upright and almost knock their heads on the low hanging rafters. With wakefulness came the realization that this was the common day for celebrating both birthdays and they looked at each other as they rolled from their blankets to the wide space between them. Clancy wore her long flannel night gown while Caleb was still clad in his buckskin breeches but was bare chested. He reached beside his covers and grabbed his tunic top and slipped it over his head, then put his feet in his moccasins. Clancy chose to descend the ladder clad as she slept. Reaching the earthen floor with her bare feet, she trotted to the fireplace and extended her arms, giving a sleepy greeting to the three watching adults seated at the table. She was soon joined by Caleb who mimicked her stance with outstretched hands seeking warmth from the curling flames.

"Well, ain't you two sumpin'! Here 'tis yore birthdays

and all you care about is warmin' yore tootsies in front o' the fire," kidded Scratch as he sipped at his coffee.

Waters and Scratch laughed together at the sight of the two sleepyheads who had turned to look at the gifts stacked on the table. The two walked to the table and looked as Waters handed matching elk-hide, hair-on possibles bags to the two. These were hand-made gifts from Scratch. High top moccasins with beaded patterns on the toe tops were given to each by Waters. After both youngsters praised the gifts and the givers, Clancy walked to a corner cabinet and reached in for Caleb's gift of the tunic while at the same time Caleb sought Clancy's gift hidden behind the door in his parent's room. When they returned and held out their gifts, both were surprised and spoke excitedly about the wondrously crafted gifts.

"Oh Caleb, these are magnificent," exclaimed Clancy as she lifted the packet of 10 matching arrows. A special painted wide band that faded from yellow to bright orange wrapped around each arrow to signify the Sun of the Morning as the owner. Each flint tipped arrow was smooth and straight and beautifully crafted.

"And this tunic, I've never had anything this beautiful!" said Caleb slowly as he examined the bead and quill work and the softness of the leather. He removed his plain buckskin top and draped the new tunic over his head slipping his hands into the fringed arms. When it was on, he ran his hands over his chest to feel the smoothness and smiled. Waters noticed how much the boy she knew had filled out through the chest and shoulders and now had the full form of a man. He stood almost as tall as his father and was nearly as broad and muscled. She knew this revealed that he would soon surpass his father in both height and size. She turned to look at Clancy and thought how she had grown and was beginning to become a full-figured woman, no longer a child. Jeremiah noticed the glaze in his wife's eyes and he was pretty sure he knew what she was thinking, as he had these same thoughts often of late.

"Clancy, how 'bout you get your outdoor clothes on cause there's somethin' else I wanna show you two," instructed Jeremiah.

Moments later, Clancy joined the family as they started out the door. The three adults preceded the youngsters and blocked the view through the door until all were standing just outside the door. Finally, Jeremiah, Waters, and Scratch stepped aside to reveal two horses tethered to the rail in front of the cabin. Standing before the birthday duo were two, beautiful Appaloosa. The near one, a stallion, was dark brown, almost black, with the pattern of white spots across his rump. Broad chested and long-limbed with a soft eye, the stallion turned and looked at Caleb as the young man reached out to touch his head. Stroking the animal's head and then his neck, he looked back at his Pa and said, "He's beautiful!"

Clancy had walked immediately to the other, a mare with the marking often referred to as a leopard. White with black spots over her entire body, she too was broad chested with a muscular rump and sturdy legs. Clancy and the mare had already become fast friends as she hugged the horse and wrapped both her arms around the mare's neck. She stroked the mare's neck, shoulders and across her back, all the while talking softly to her new horse. Stepping to the side of the mare, she unloosed the tether and grabbing a handful of mane, she stepped back and swung a leg high, pulling herself atop the mare.

Looking down at Caleb, she said, "Race ya!" Turning her mount's head, she kicked her with her heels and headed up the trail that led through the trees to the upper meadow where the rest of their horses were held.

Caught by surprise, Caleb didn't hesitate to also mount his horse bareback and turned to follow the rapidly disappearing Clancy. Leaning down along the neck of his mount he spoke to his new horse as he dug his heels into his sides. The horse seemed to lunge and with long strides soon overtook the fleeing girl who now turned to see the charging stallion and again gigged her horse for more speed. When the two arrived at the edge of the meadow, Clancy was only ahead by a neck length and she squealed with delight at the excitement of the race.

It was just a short while when the birthday duo returned to the cabin and greeted the expectant group with excited chatter and exclamations of the qualities and beauty of their new horses. Jeremiah turned to Waters and Scratch and said, "I think they like 'em, don't you?"

A TONE OF EXCITEMENT FILLED THE AIR AS the busy village began to hum with activity that told of preparations for their move to summer grounds. Word quickly spread through the village that this summer they would camp near another band of Arapaho with family members that had married into that band. They also anticipated seeing several other close friends. It was not unusual for different bands to camp near one another for additional strength in the event of attack and for greater numbers for large buffalo hunts. When the huge, migrating monsters of the plains moved, the dust from the herd could block out the sun for days and the numbers could not be counted even if one stood on a promontory for a week.

Caleb wound his way through the maze of lodges and the beehive of activity on his way to visit his grandfather and to seek his counsel. The questions that had been bothering him were brought to the forefront of his mind during the recent hunt with the older men and the conversation around the fire. Their words were little help to the confusion that swirled around his head these days, and the young man was hoping the shaman of the village, his grandfather Black Kettle, could give him some direction.

As he made his way to the central lodge, he passed many families busy with their preparations and several eligible young women smiled at him as he walked by. He knew all the members of the village and had often spoken with Dancing Dove and Little Flower, but never thought of them in any way but as friends and fellow members of the village. Yet, their smiles said their thoughts had been much more personal. In the eyes of the other young people of the village, He Who Talks with the Wind, had become a man and his long blonde hair and broad shoulders set him apart from others his age. He was a proven hunter and was considered by all as a warrior of considerable honor.

"Greetings Grandfather, I have come seeking your counsel. Have you time for your student and grandson?" asked the young man with expectancy in his voice. Black Kettle, like the rest of the village, would need to prepare for the move to summer grounds but Caleb was hopeful for some guidance.

"I always have time for He Who Talks With the Wind. How can I help you, my son?"

The two, separated by many years but closer still by common loves, seated themselves opposite each other with the remains of the morning cook fire between them. Both were attired in buckskin tunics, but Black Kettle wore leggings, moccasins and breechcloth while Caleb had buckskin breeches. Although not related by blood, the two were closely knit by many interests and studied subjects.

Caleb began, "I'm confused. My mind has been tying itself in knots trying to figure out what I'm supposed to be doing and what I'm supposed to be feeling," he paused, and picking up a nearby stick, poked at the glowing coals of the fire. Looking up at the wise old man, he continued, "One time I think I should be courtin' Clancy, Sun of the Morning, and thinkin' 'bout getting' married. And the next, I'm thinkin' about takin' off on my own and maybe goin' back to the white man's world or maybe hookin' up with some trappin' outfit and heading to the high mountains to chase after beaver. It just seems I should have more direction to my life!" he stated with an unusual degree of exasperation. The old man sat patiently and waited for the young man to continue.

With nothing else forthcoming, Black Kettle began, "I see, so you are feeling just what every young man feels at this time in his life."

"I am? Well, that don't make it any easier. I still don't know what to do!"

"And it is not my place to tell you what to do. This is something you must discover for yourself," stated the Shaman.

"But how do I do that?"

"It is not an easy thing, and with each young person it is different. Many of our young men and sometimes, women will go on what some call a Vision Quest."

"I've heard of that, but what is it exactly?" inquired Caleb.

"With proper preparation and guidance, one would go alone to a special place and spend the time seeking the direction you long for by waiting on the Great Spirit, or Manitou, to give that guidance."

With a frown of frustration, Caleb replied, "But our religion is different from yours. We try to follow what the Good Book says, you know, worshiping God and all."

"Yes, I know. I understand about the white man's God and the one they call Jesus. I don't know, but what you call God and what we call Manitou or the Great Spirit are not the same. But that is not for me to say. I believe that if you decided to go on a Vision Quest it would not be different than what some of your people do. Some of your people also go away by themselves and wait for their God to give them direction."

"Hmmm . . . that's somethin' to think about, all right. Maybe that's what I'll have to do," surmised the young man. Thanking his grandfather, the two men grasped forearms and Caleb rose to leave.

Sitting at the table with both hands grasping the cold coffee cup, Jeremiah looked at Waters standing before the window and watching something outside. He always marveled at the beauty of his mate, he never thought he could be so blessed as to have a woman as beautiful and intelligent as Laughing Waters. Looking at her and thinking of their time together, he thought of the two youngsters that were their adopted children. He thought about his recent conversation with Caleb and chuckled.

Turning back to her husband, Waters asked, "What are you laughing about?"

"Oh, just thinking about a recent talk I had with Caleb. He's kinda flustered about his feelings and all. He's growin' up mighty fast, that boy is."

"Was this conversation anything about a certain young woman we both know? Maybe like the conversation I had with Clancy?" inquired Waters with a smile poking dimples in her cheeks.

"What are we gonna do 'bout them two? They're actin' just like we did when we were their age, and that kinda scares me a little," stated Jeremiah with a bit of mischievousness showing.

"I've been thinking about that. Let me tell you what I think," said Waters watching her husband for some response. But he wisely held his tongue and gave her his attention.

"Let's send them on a hunt together. Maybe down towards South Pass to see if they can get any stray buffalo."

"Alone? Together? That'd take at least a week, maybe longer. Do you know what you're sayin' woman?"

"Yes. And I always know what I'm saying, unlike somebody else I know," she stated as she stood with both hands on her hips. She continued, "I think a trip like that will make them think a bit more about being together in the long term. I think it'll either bring them closer together or drive them apart. Either way, they'll be thinking a little clearer when they come back."

"I'm glad somebody'll be thinkin' clearer," grumbled Jeremiah. "What about the move for the village?"

"That will make the hunt easier. They can go on the hunt and come back to the summer camp. That will give them more time for the hunt, if needed, and a shorter haul back."

What she said made sense to Jeremiah, but the usual constraints of the white man's world gave him pause as he considered her suggestion. Surrendering his will and doubts, and without any other possible direction, he decided to condescend to his wife. His thoughts were interrupted by the opening door and the entrance of the subject of their discussion.

"Hi Pa, Hi Ma, boy you two look awful serious. What's wrong?" asked Caleb as he sat in his usual place at the table. Without getting a response, he plunged ahead with another question, "Did you ever go on a vision quest?" directing his question at his father then turning to Waters asked the same question with his facial expression.

Jeremiah answered, "No, neither one of us did. But there were several in the village that went on one. Shield went on a quest, didn't he?" Jeremiah directed the question to his wife.

"Yes, but you will need to ask him about it. Sometimes those that go do not discuss the quest. It is personal between them and the Great Spirit."

Before Caleb could comment, Jeremiah interjected with, "But we've got something else for you to do before you go on a vision quest. We think you and Clancy should go on a buffalo hunt."

"Really? When, where, and who else?"

"Just you and Clancy, taking the two mules for

packin', and ridin' your new horses, of course," shared Jeremiah, knowing the excitement his son felt. For the two young people to be entrusted with such a major task was evidence of the considerable trust and confidence Jeremiah and Waters held for them.

"Have you told Clancy?" asked Caleb as he stood and headed for the door.

"No, you can tell her and then you'll need to begin making preparations," replied Jeremiah.

Leaping from the door and off the stoop, Caleb ran to the corrals where he last saw Clancy to share the news of the anticipated hunt. As he disappeared, Waters walked to the still open door and pushed it closed. Turning to Jeremiah, she smiled, walked to his side and seated herself on his lap, and said, "That also means we'll be alone while they're gone."

"Alone, are you kidding me. Not only do we have Little John, but we'll be on the move with the entire village! That's not what I call alone!"

Hearing the news of the planned hunt, Clancy and Caleb excitedly chattered about the trip and all the preparations necessary. They talked about supplies, weapons, location, anticipated results and much more. Clancy looked at Caleb with a grin and said, "I betcha I get the first buffler."

"Hah! Only if I letcha! You ain't never been after buffler before and they're not like those puny elk you got last time."

"Yeah, the elk I got and you didn't, remember?" she jibed.

With all the thoughts and preparations for the hunt, no longer were their minds focused on themselves or each other. Direction for their energies focused on this anticipated experience of a lifetime. Just the thought of finally being old enough and experienced enough to go on a hunt without the older warriors was somewhat overwhelming but also confidence building. The remainder of the day was spent gathering and packing supplies and checking and double checking for needed items.

Jeremiah guided Caleb with most of the supply selection and Waters aided Clancy with the finer details of food supply. When the two women entered the cabin on another search for last minute items, Waters drew Clancy toward the bedroom and reached under the bed drawing out a white tanned and beaded scabbard. Extending it to Clancy, she said, "This is the Hawken my husband brought me from his trip back East. I have not used it very much, but you will need it for buffalo. May the Spirit guide you as you hunt."

"Oh my, are you sure Ma? This is an amazing rifle, it's just like Pa's and Caleb's," she observed.

"Yes, it is, and yes I'm sure. You have shown you are a good hunter and you know how to use this rifle. You will do well, my child."

Thanking her adopted mother, she reached her arms around the woman and gave her a long loving hug. Pulling away, she looked into Water's eyes and said, "This is a special hunt in more ways than one, am I right?"

"Yes, my child. Trust the Great Spirit, or your God, to guide you and keep you safe."

She nodded her head and turned away to place the rifle by the door for the morrow's departure. The night passed all too slowly but without fail, the grey light of early morning bid the youngsters a cheerful greeting of promise. After a morning feast of fried elk liver and gravy ladled over sourdough biscuits, the two were ready to start the journey. Final preparations and packing done, they mounted the spotted horses, grabbed the lead ropes of the two mules and bid their Ma and Pa goodbye.

A bright blue sky framed the two as they rode into the lower reaches of the valley and started the descent on the trail below. They turned and waved just before they dropped out of sight on the trail through the scrub oak and buck brush. Caleb turned in his saddle to look at Clancy and smiled saying, "This is gonna be a great hunt, I can feel it in my bones," he stated as he echoed the common expression of Scratch. But the excitement did not outweigh the trepidation the stirred the spirits of the two adventuresome hunters.

"THAT'S THE FINAL WORD! THERE'S NO SENSE in arguin' 'bout it. We got together and decided it's best for the whole outfit. There's been too much sickness and we gotta stop this Cholera somehow and this is the way we decided. You already buried one of your number, now your two wagons got 'nuff guns and shooters you shouldn't have any truck with injuns and sech," stated Macklin McCormick, the burly leader of the wagon train that showed plenty of activity as they prepared to continue to South Pass. "Mebbe, you'll luck out and the rest of yore bunch'll heal up and you can join us at Fort Bridger. That's about a week or so on down the trail."

"That ain't right, you leavin' us here. Why, my woman is sick 'n mebbe dyin' and so too wit' da Martinez' folks. Ain't Christian, I tell ya. You bunch o' Mormons always spoutin' yore Bible and stuff, fine lot you are. If I weren't feelin' so poorly myself, I'd tear right into the bunch o' ya. Ain't a one of ya's man enuff to tote my pack!" boasted

Braxton Jefferson, the big barrel-chested leader of the scraggly bunch that stood behind him.

The Jefferson wagon had been allowed to join the Mormon train at the behest of Mrs. Jefferson's sister and brother-in-law, who were back-door relation to the Brigham Young family, or at least they claimed to be. But the entire Jefferson family didn't take to the rules and religion of the train and were often in conflict with many of the travelers. Usually, because the Jefferson's were a profane, lazy and dirty bunch that had a habit of bullying anyone that disagreed with them. There had been many arguments and several fights with the usual outcome showing nothing resolved and additional disagreements fermenting.

Cholera had already claimed twelve lives, the most recent, Louisa Jefferson, the only daughter of the Jeffersons, and the constant recurrence had baffled the many members of the wagon train. Some thought it was a contagious disease and the only way to put a stop to it was to isolate the presumed carriers. Because the ones usually stricken were the stragglers and those late to camp, it was presumed that they bore the disease and spread it among the others.

It would not be for some time that it they would discover that the primary cause was tainted water. When a camp was made, the best sites would be taken by the leaders and that would usually be on the upstream side of the water source. With little sanitation practices, the downstream campers drank the tainted water and suffered debilitating symptoms of diarrhea, vomiting, dehydration and even death. Cholera was a common affliction for wagon trains as they followed the North Platte River of the Oregon Trail due to the limited water sources and oft-used camps that polluted the water supplies.

To the relief of McCormick and the other leaders of the wagon train, Braxton Jefferson signaled to his sons and the Martinez boy to follow him back to the wagon. As he turned away he said, "We don't need them anyway, we'll get along without 'em and we can make better time anyhow."

The wagons were a scout train for the Mormons, sent by Brigham Young, to ensure the Oregon trail and the proposed cutoff to their chosen land, which would later become known as the Mormon trail, would be passable for the many wagons that were to follow. Numbering just eighteen wagons, it was small in comparison to the numbers that would come over the Oregon trail in later years, but it was a sizeable group for this early in the season.

They were headed over South Pass and on to Fort Bridger for re-supply. From the Fort they would scout out a more Northerly route that would take them to the heart of their promised land. In an attempt to escape the Cholera outbreak, the wagon master had taken the train further north than usual, and was now doubling back along what would later be known as the Red Canyon trail.

He knew they had lost a few days with this detour, but the search for fresh water would often make it neces-sary to vary the traveled trail. It had been magnanimous of them to allow the Jefferson's to join them, but they were also relieved to be rid of the troublesome bunch. Leaving their camp at the edge of the timber in the foothills of the Wind River Range, they anticipated starting their ascent of South Pass by mid-day. The hill-sides were showing an abundance of red clay and rim-rock of red stone lined the edges of the flat-top plateau before them.

"Boys, you take Miguel with you and scout around some. See if you cain't get us some fresh meat o' some kind. Yore Ma could use some good eatin' and so could I fer that matter. Miguel, you check on yore Ma n' Pa 'fore ya go. Lazarus'll stay here with us to take care o' the mules," sounded orders from the thick bushy beard of the big Braxton Jefferson. He was used to ordering others around and wouldn't tolerate any backtalk. With a grunt and mumbles, he crawled into the back of the wagon saying, "Move over woman, you ain't the only one sick."

Colby Jefferson was a slightly scaled down model of his father who was also a bully and a braggart who didn't bathe any more often than his smelly dad. The main difference between them; where Braxton had a bushy batch of whiskers, Colby was still cultivating his two or three stubby chin hairs which was typical for a sixteen-year-old.

Cormick, two years younger, resembled his mother but still bore the look of the Jefferson patriarch. Dark hair, broad shoulders, but slighter of build and narrower through the hip. He had a quiet manner about him and his eyes were green like his mother, Eliza, and she catered to him because of the resemblance. Miguel Martinez was the only child of Ricardo and Maria, and with fifteen years behind him, he was full grown by most standards. Standing just under six feet, his lean frame was well-attired in black trousers and matching black waist length jacket, his black hair was topped with a flat-brimmed black hat with a silver, concho hat band. He was a handsome figure of a young man with coal black eyes peering out from beneath thin black eyebrows and a smile that flashed bright white teeth.

The opposite of the Jeffersons, Miguel took pride in his appearance. But the personalities of the three blended well in their many trouble-making schemes. Early afternoon showed the three unsuccessful hunters returning to the campsite with the two wagons. The only activity was the big black slave that curried the mules as he hummed an old spiritual that spoke of "Canaan land."

The stench from the campsite assaulted the returnees' nostrils and prompted exclamations of disgust. "Whoooooeeeee, this place stinks! Lazarus, hook up them mules, there's another stream not too far south of here and we can camp there. Maybe the fresh water'll help ever'body an' we'll get away from this stinkin' place. It smells like somebody fell in an outhouse, climbed out, caught a skunk and shook all the stink right outta him!"

Receiving no argument from his fellow hunters and no movement from the wagons, Colby continued, "Come on, get a move on you lazy nigra!" Cormick cast a sideways glance at the unmarked grave of their sister and turned his horse away from the camp calling to his brother, "I'll go 'head on and get us a campsite in the trees by that stream. I saw a place this mornin', I think'll do just right." Digging his heels into his horse's ribs, he trotted away from the wagons before Colby could countermand him.

Two hours later, Cormick sat on his mount with one leg hooked around the saddle horn as he waited for the wagons. At the edge of a cluster of cottonwoods, he looked back over his shoulder toward his selected camp. It would not be easily seen from the trail and would provide good cover for the time they'd spend before returning to the trek after everyone recovered.

Spotting the wagons trailing Colby, he saw Lazarus was driving their wagon and Miguel was handling the mules on their wagon. *Hmmm, guess Pa's not feelin' too good cause it ain't like him to ride in a wagon. He always said wagons were fer wimmin and kids. Looks like Miguel's folks ain't doin' too good either. Oh well, maybe a few days in a new camp will help ever'body,* mused Cormick. As the wagons neared, Cormick called out to his brother, "Ain't Pa feelin' good?"

"Don't guess so, I didn't bother 'em. Just let 'em sleep," he stated as the wagon drew alongside his brother. "He's easier to get along with when he's sleepin' anyway," he whispered. Cormick motioned the wagons to follow him as they cut across the unmarked soil and sagebrush. Behind them the rising bluff of red clay was framed by red and tan sandstone rimrock that sheltered the lengthy valley. Marked only by cactus, rocks, sagebrush and an occasional scurrying jack rabbit, the prairie-like plains of the valley slowly gave way to the juniper, pinion and cedar of the lowlands.

As the scrub brush yielded to the cottonwoods of the water fed draw, a clearing revealed itself as the new campsite. A slight bluff rose behind them and a bit of a drop-off that obscured the trunks but not the tops of a smattering of cottonwood and willows revealed a nearby stream. Colby nodded his head in approval, seeing the cluster of taller cottonwoods that provided good shade for their camp. "Good choice, brother."

THE DYING COOK FIRES GLOWED IN THE shadows as the flames gave way to the coals that fought for life under the grey ashes and charcoal remains of burnt wood. Some of the fire circles held the presence of blanket-clad family members with glazed over eyes hiding secrets of plans and dreams seldom shared.

With two days' travel behind them, the members of the village were still fueled by hopes for the summer camp and the anticipated neighbors from the other band of the Arapaho, or as they would say, *Inun-ina* (*people of our own kind*). Yet, they referred to themselves as *Hinono'eino* (*our people*). It was common that families would have relatives that had married into the other bands and most were anxious to be reunited, if only for the summer. Some even anticipated new acquaintances and friends and, of course, the young people had romantic notions they hoped to fulfill.

Some of the cook fires were rekindled to small warming fires as blanket covered mounds surrounded the low-burning flames. Night covered the surrounding pines and shrouded the camping village with the security of darkness. Jeremiah and Waters sat by their fire as Scratch sat across from them. The unusual silence brought a touch of melancholy and thoughts of absent family members.

"Are you not concerned about our two children?" asked Waters as she turned to Jeremiah.

"Look woman, this was your idea, so I don't know what you're concerned about. They've been out hunting before, besides, I'm pretty sure Clancy can take care of Caleb if she has too," he said, trying to keep the smile from spreading across his fire-lit face.

The anticipated laughter brought a comic relief to her expression as she pushed her shoulder against his and responded, "Well, I am glad you finally see that we women can take care of you men as we so often are called upon to do. Our Sun of the Morning does have a good head on her shoulders and will keep our son from doing something foolish. You are right, I should not be concerned, but as a mother of two young people that did not come from my belly, I will be concerned if I want to and you cannot stop me," she stated with conviction.

"Wal, I shore taught him better. He's s'posed to know it don't do no good to argue with a woman. 'Specially the one that cooks his food and takes care of his house," crowed the scrawny Scratch as he poked at the fire with a stick.

"So now the both of you are gangin' up on me? If that ain't a fine how do you do." Looking at Waters he noticed the somber expression that held more than she was sharing and he asked, "What is it? There's something else bothering you, what's goin' on?"

"It's my father, he looks like he has aged so much just this past winter. He told me that after we get to our summer camp, he wanted me to take over his Shaman duties. I think he is planning on going away."

Black Kettle had been the medicine man and leader of the village for many years and had done his best to groom Waters to take his place, though she had expressed her reluctance. At the beginning of the past winter, he had yielded his leadership of the village to his nephew, Broken Shield, and if he was now desirous of making Waters the Shaman, it would mean he was planning on going away. Yet when an elder spoke of 'going away' he meant he would go into the wilderness to meet with his Great Spirit and let the Spirit take him to the other side. It was the way of the people not to burden their family with the last days of their life and their death. These were the thoughts that weighed heavily on the heart of Waters as she thought of her father.

Jeremiah remained silent. There were no words that would relieve the burden being borne by his beloved. The way of the people was ingrained in each subsequent generation and was honored by every member of the family and the village. Although Waters had a natural talent for healing and knew the many herbs and plants used in the traditional remedies, it was a tremendous responsibility to be entrusted with the honor as the village Shaman.

It was an honor that also carried the burden of leadership as a member of the tribal council and, if need be, as a successor of leadership for the village. It was an unusual thing for that position to be held by a woman, even a proven and respected warrior like Laughing Waters. But Jeremiah was certain the honor and responsibility was not what weighed on her now, but rather thoughts of her father and his waning health and time remaining.

The winking of the star light signaled the retreat of darkness as it yielded to the gradual light of the morning. Dirt was kicked onto the dying embers of the remaining cook fires as the village began its morning trek toward the summer grounds. Leading the convoy of lodge-laden travois, dogs bearing small packs, and families on horseback and walking, was Broken Shield astride his paint stallion beside Jeremiah on his steel dust gelding.

The two leaders had been friends since childhood and had shared many an adventure together. Shield had been with Jeremiah when the two young men and Waters had started the vengeance quest after the killers of Jeremiah's adopted father, Ezekiel. Jeremiah had joined Shield as the two battled both the Blackfeet and the Crow before founding their winter camp in the Absaroka. This bond of blood and years was unbreakable and bound the two together in every endeavor and challenge.

Following the two men, Waters led the blue roan that bore the travois and their buffalo hide lodge while Shield's wife, Pine Leaf, the Crow war leader and pipe bearer, led their pack horses with travois and packs. Scratch had left early and together with the warrior, White Horse, scouted the trail ahead and doubled as a hunter for meat for the travelers. This would be a long day of travel and the summer grounds would not be gained for at least two more days.

The trail between the Wind River and the foothills to the South West was an oft traveled route yet, because of the terrain, there were many ravines, gullies and bluffs to circumvent. What could be covered by a single man on horseback in two or three days would take close to a week for the caravan of villagers to cover. Shield had chosen to take a higher trail that took them into the black timber of the foothills. As the sage and cactus flats gave way to the Pinion, Juniper and Cedar of the foothills, the trail soon led them into the black timber cresting the smaller hillsides.

As Broken Shield and White Wolf, or Jeremiah, rode side by side at the head of the column, Jeremiah shared Water's concerns with his friend. "My wife has been concerned for her father and a little apprehensive about the responsibility as Shaman that would fall to her if he leaves us."

"I share her burden. Waters has always been my sister in many ways though we did not have the same father, and I know how she feels about this. Black Kettle has been like a father to me as well and I have great respect for his decision about this matter of Shaman. I think though, that he is just preparing her. I do not believe he will leave us soon," responded Shield.

"Did he tell you that or are you just guessing?"

"Not a guess, but more a thought. He will not go easily to the other side and the land of our fathers. There is still much he wants to do. He has said he wants to spend some more time with your son, Talks to the Wind."

"Yeah, he and Caleb have a special bond. I think it would be good for both of them to have some time together. His grandfather spent some time with him when he was making the gift for Clancy and Caleb couldn't stop talking about the things he learned. Yeah, it would be good for them," surmised Jeremiah.

The sudden whisper of an arrow passing just in front of them stopped the two leaders instantly. Turning to look uphill at the source as he started to draw his Hawken from its scabbard, Jeremiah's hand was stopped as Shield pointed to White Horse standing uphill beside a tall ponderosa and signaling a stop. Without hesitation, Shield turned and gave a hand signal to those following to immediately stop and remain silent. White Horse trotted down the hill to the side of Shield and spoke softly to his chief, "There is a small party of Cheyenne just below the tree line. They are moving toward the river and I do not believe they spotted the dust of our people."

With a signal for Jeremiah to follow, the leader dropped from his mount and gave the reins to both his and his friend's horses before moving from the trail to a better vantage point. About fifty yards downhill from the trail, a slight clearing in the trees revealed a promontory of boulders that afforded a good view of the valley below them. Bellying up to the top of the boulder, the two men observed a Cheyenne party of a dozen warriors.

"They're still moving away, I think they're crossing the valley and the river," whispered Jeremiah.

Shield nodded his head silently and surveyed the valley before them. The hillside they were on was covered with black timber and provided good cover for the Arapaho movers. The hillside dropped off a bluff edge and leveled out into sage brush covered plains before another slight drop off near the river bank. The river channel was thick with cottonwood, willows, alders and occasional aspen that afforded a swath of green that cut the valley of brown soil and blue-grey sagebrush.

The Cheyenne were usually friendly with the Arapaho, but any party that size was bound to have a few hotheaded, anxious young men desirous of proving their mettle as warriors and would eagerly seek an opportunity for honors in battle. The twelve Cheyenne would be greatly outnumbered by the number of warriors in this band of Arapaho, but any conflict with the entire village involved could result in unnecessary bloodshed. Shield did not want to deal with any conflict during this move to summer grounds.

"We will wait before we move again. I want you and Scratch and White Horse to stay back and watch them," he said nodding toward the Cheyenne, "and I will send them with your horse. After we move out, you three stay and watch the back trail as you follow. I will pass the word for two more warriors to stay and wait for you."

Jeremiah nodded his head in assent and turned to watch the retreating Cheyenne as Shield moved away. While he waited, the Cheyenne continued on course toward the river and Jeremiah knew it would take about an hour before they would reach the river bottom. Scratch and White Horse soon joined Jeremiah on the large boulder and lay prone beside the larger man. As Jeremiah returned his gaze toward the Cheyenne, two scouts of the hunting party split off from the group and gigged their horses in separate directions. Motioning to Scratch, he softly spoke to his friend, "Looks like they're gonna scout out the river bottom." But as he spoke, one scout turned his mount and started for the foothills where the trail used by the Arapaho lay sheltered in the black timber.

"If that'n keeps goin' the way he is, he'll cross our trail certain sure," observed the crusty mountain man.

"He mighta seen some dust or sumpin' and he's gonna have a closer look, course, it were'nt too far from there that we came up from the river," he continued.

Without taking his eyes from the slow moving scout, Jeremiah said to Scratch, "If he keeps comin' we'll need to head him off down the trail," then turning to the warrior beside them, "White Horse, you stay here and keep watch on the rest of that party. If they cross the river, then you can come up and join us. Scratch, you and I will get those two warriors Shield left behind, and we'll set up an ambush for that scout down the trail."

With the plan made, the two friends snaked their way off the boulder to set things in motion. Retrieving their mounts from the trees, they mounted up and worked their way back up the slope to the trail and the waiting warriors. After uniting, the four men rode the back trail looking for a likely ambush site. Within less than a half mile, the trail passed through some thick timber of Douglas fir and Engelmann Spruce.

Speaking low, Jeremiah directed Scratch to take one of the warriors and take shelter above the trail, then motioned for the other Arapaho to join him as they moved below the path. With horses tethered further back in the trees, the four men took up positions that would provide both good cover and good views of the trail. Knowing the wait would not be long if the Cheyenne came up the trail as anticipated, each man took a comfortable position to await the action.

The scuffing of hooves on the softened trail gave little warning, but to the attentive Jeremiah, he knew the Cheyenne was near. Signaling his compatriots, he lifted his rifle to his shoulder and brought it to full cock with a muffled click. Apparently unheard by the approaching scout, the sounds of footfalls continued. Within moments, the Cheyenne warrior appeared on the trail with his eyes downcast reading the sign on the trail below him. Jeremiah stepped into the trail with uplifted rifle and spoke firmly with a "Ho!" that stopped the scout instantly.

With only a knife and tomahawk within easy reach, the warrior's eyes grew wide and flared with anger. His bow was unstrung and in the quiver on his back and he fingered the handle on the tomahawk. With a motion of his rifle, Jeremiah shook his head and directed the warrior's attention to the other three men of the ambush. As he looked from man to man, the Cheyenne released his grip on his tomahawk and crossed his hands on the neck of his horse. Surprisingly he spoke to Jeremiah in English, "White man, you travel with these Arapaho?"

"I live with the people. They are my people," answered Jeremiah. "Why do you follow us? The Cheyenne are not enemies of the Arapaho."

"I look for woman. Our village only has old and fat women. I want a young woman."

Smiling at this response, Jeremiah countered, "Why would a young and pretty Arapaho want to be with you, a Cheyenne?"

"Like you said, we are not enemies. If I had a young woman, we could be really good friends," he said showing white teeth behind a broad grin.

All four of the ambuscade chuckled at the Cheyenne's remark and Jeremiah spoke, "Well here's what'chur gonna do. You're gonna turn around and go back to your party and not follow us anymore. We have a big village and we're joinin' up with another so I don't think you'd wanna tangle with us, understand?" receiving a nod from the lone warrior, he continued. "An' iffn' you're wantin' a woman, you best come back later with a peace party and maybe you can join in the courtin' if they'll have you."

With an enthusiastic nod and a broad smile, the young warrior turned his mount and dug his heels into the horse's ribs to lope back down the trail to rejoin his party. With another chuckle and a motion of his arms, Jeremiah had the others join him as they gathered the horses and started back on the trail to a reunion with the Arapaho village.

THE CRYSTALLINE SPARKLES RADIATED THEIR brilliance against the deep black of the night sky, keeping watch over the tired travelers now supine with hands under their heads and eyes wide to take in the splendor of the heavens. Wrapped in their reflections, they were silent for several moments until Clancy's muted question pierced the darkness. "What about the future? What do you want to do or go or..." Her spoken thoughts trailed off into the silence. Rolling to her side and looking across the dying embers of their cook-fire, she narrowed her eyes to see if Caleb was still awake.

His slow response reassured her, "I've been thinkin' about it a lot lately," after a short pause, he continued, "and I don't know. One minute I think I got it all figgered out, and the next I'm as confused as ever. What'chu been thinkin'?"

"Oh, 'bout the same I guess," as she rolled onto her back to look again heavenward, "when I look at all those stars, I think about my Mum and Da and how they used to look at them. When we were comin' out on the wagon train, they'd roll the bonnet back on the wagon, and we'd just lay there an' look at the stars and talk about nothin' special. They were always happy together like that."

During the past three days of their journey, Caleb and Clancy had spoken very little except about the coming hunt. While both had similar thoughts troubling them, they chose to let the unspoken remain hidden within. Now the conversation was beginning to touch on more tender thoughts, thoughts neither considered themselves ready to deal with, but that was part of what this trip was all about, an opportunity to really talk things out and maybe get direction for their lives. But what circles around in your mind and what comes out in words can often be quite different. And which one would directly confront the subject of their future together, and was there one? The silence was heavy upon them.

"Sometimes I think of us, you and me, like that. You know, like my Mum and Da or even like Jeremiah and Waters. Do you?" asked Clancy.

"Do I what?"

"Think of us like that, you know, happy together."

Remembering the many times, he had pictured them together like Jeremiah and Waters, a smile tugged at his face in the dark, but he looked towards Clancy to see if she had seen his expression. "Yeah, I guess so, I mean, well, yeah I have," and held his breath to hear her response. He never thought he could talk to her like this, but it seemed natural somehow.

"You don't sound so sure about it. What else have you been thinkin' about, I mean, like for your life and stuff?"

He sat up and crossed his arms in front of his knees, leaning his chin on his forearm as he looked at the blanket shrouded form across the fire ring. "Sometimes I think about going back to the white man's world, you know the city or something, kinda like where I came from back in Michigan territory. But I don't know what we'd do there, you know, how we'd live. Cause I don't know nothin' 'bout farmin' or anything like that. Or in the city, I guess I could get a job, but where'd we live?"

She noticed his expressions and dreams included her with his use of 'we' and 'us' when he spoke. The thought gave her a warmth and a touch of fear of the unknown as well. "Well, have you thought about just stayin' here in the high lonesome with our folks? They seem to get along all right here in the mountains. I like it too, but I never thought I would. Sometimes I think about the other world out there, you know, with our own people in the settlements too, but, I don't know," she ended her comment with a sigh of frustration.

"Yeah, I know what you mean. When I'm with you Clancy, I'm happy. Like now, when it's just us, it's special. I've never talked with anyone like this before. I just can't see us not bein' together. But when we're not together, my thoughts seem to run off by themselves and I'm either in the woods huntin' or ridin' my horse through the valley and up the mountains and I'm by myself. But, when I'm not with you, I want to be with you, even though sometimes you irritate me, and I wanna turn you over my knee and spank you like my Pa used to spank me!"

"Spank me? You just try it, buster! And what do you mean irritate you?"

"I don't know, like when we're in the village and the others look at you and you act like you like it and such."

The smile that split her face revealed itself to Caleb with the reflection of the dim light on her white teeth. The moon had crawled out from its hiding place behind the low lying clouds just above the horizon and now gave a warm glow to their campsite. She knew jealousy when she saw it and was touched by his admission of the age-old emotion. Quietly she replied, "They don't mean anything to me, you should know that."

"Yeah, well . . ."

"Don't you think I feel the same way when Little Flower and Cactus Bloom smile at you the way they do? Cactus is well named, she'd just as soon stick you as not," she said with a bit of a pout that did not go unnoticed by Caleb.

"I never noticed them. They look at me like that, huh?"

He saw the stick flying at him just in time to duck his head and let it fly behind him. With a chuckle he said, "Sides, they're just kids, not a woman like you."

Lying back down and turning her back to him, she said, "We need to get some sleep if we're getting an early start tomorrow." The hidden smile warmed her with the thoughts expressed by Caleb. *He really does want to be with me. Maybe we could be happy together like my Mum and Da and like Ma and Pa. Yeah, I could be happy with him,* she thought as she pulled the blanket over her shoulder.

Caleb stretched out on his robe and again placed his hands behind his head and gazed at the Milky Way overhead. *That looks like a trail through the heavens. Maybe that's the trail we're supposed to take together. Yeah, I can see that.*

The red and tan sandstone rimrock above them trailed off with red clay soil dropping down to the valley below. This formation was like a line drawn by the Creator that marked the boundary of the Wind River mountain range. It was as if He had said, *"This far and no farther."*

The two hunters approached the Popo Agie creek just before noon and decided to take their mid-day break on the banks of the willow clad stream. The trail that followed this stream uphill through the cut between the foothills would take them past the sinks and lead them to the previous summer camps of the Arapaho and would also bring them near the original cabin. But their journey was to find buffalo and bring the meat back to the family and village. The valley that spread out below was green with the early spring buds and shoots from the cotton-woods and willows as well as the many grasses and flowers that chased the stream into the flats.

Now dismounted and seated on a grassy slope below the shady cottonwood, the two sat a little closer together and shared bits of pemmican and watched the small fire warm the coffeepot. The animals with loosened cinches grazed on the fresh sprouts of grass and basked in the warm sunlight. The chuckling of the stream sang in harmony with the song of the yellow breasted mead-owlark perched on a branch overhead. Both young people just smiled at each other and took in the beauty that surrounded them. Conversation was unnecessary as they both recalled the shared thoughts of the night before. It was as if a mutual decision had been made and they were to look to the future together.

"Couple years ago, just down below there, we got a couple o' buffalo. But from here, it don't look like there's any o' them shaggies around," shared Caleb, bringing their thoughts back to the task at hand.

"So, where we gonna look for 'em now?" asked Clancy as she leaned over to rub Two Bits behind his ears. Her faithful companion, the big black dog that could be mistaken for a black bear, seldom left her side.

"We'll cross over there," he said as he motioned to the South at a ridge rising from the rimrock, "there's another little valley that game likes to hang out in, cuz there's a good waterin' hole. We'll have a looksee there and if no luck, then we'll come back and follow this red canyon down aways. There's usually some woolies that like to hang out along here even through the winter and there might be some taking their leisure what with the new grass and such."

Mid-afternoon found the two hunters belly down on a slight knoll overlooking the bottom of the narrow valley. The small stream in the bottom was fed by high country snow melt and ran muddy through the bottom. The grassy area was littered with a small herd of shaggy brown beasts that lazily grazed near the overflowing stream. With a cloudless sky, the sun shone bright on the backs of the buckskin clad duo that watched sanguine gathering below. Waiting for a closer shot, they slipped back below the rise and lay on their sides facing each other.

"I think if we give 'em a spell, they'll work down this-away and we'll get a better shot. But we can't wait too long, cuz we'll need enough daylight to do the butcherin'," stated Caleb. Clancy looked at the young man with expectant eyes and thought of the times they had hunted together before. She was always amazed at the knowledge garnered by this young man in his short years, but she was proud of him in a way she didn't really understand.

Sometimes they were competitive in their hunting endeavors, but this time was more of camaraderie and enjoying the time together. Her thoughts had taken a romantic turn in the recent months of contemplation, maybe it was just the way of a young woman, but she thought it to be more of the way with the two of them together. It seemed they had always been together and were meant to be together forever, but somewhere there tugged a bit of doubt that she didn't understand. With these thoughts spinning around in her mind, she missed what Caleb said and she asked, "What'd you say?"

"I said, I think I hear them gruntin' and it sounds like they're gittin' close. Let's take a look." He bellied up to the crest to get a better view as Clancy followed suit. At the edge of the small herd, a couple of young bulls were sparring and had worked their way closer to the mound.

"As soon as they are separate enough, and we can both get a shot, we'll take it," directed Caleb.

"Which one do I take?" asked Clancy as she observed the dust-up with the bulls.

"You're on my left, take the one on the left, but wait till I say," instructed the young man.

Just moments later, the two young bulls backed away

from the skirmish and dropped their heads as if to graze. "Now!"

With the roar of a single shot, both Hawkens spewed their grey smoke and hurtled the round balls of lead across the intervening distance to bury themselves in the shaggy coats of the two bulls. Dust blossomed low on the sides of the buffalo as the bullets sought blood just behind the front leg in the low chest of each animal. A grunt and a bellow moved both animals forward with the far one dropping as if poleaxed and the nearer one staggering for three uncertain steps and falling over as if a sail was pushed by a strong gale.

Heads of the other buffalo came up as they sought the source of the disturbing noise and confusion clouded their eyes as they deliberated on their flight, but as a big cow snorted, the herd was spurred to action and began to trot away from the smoke and noise. Before moving from their place, both hunters reloaded their rifles then walked slowly toward the downed beasts. One leg on the close bull moved as if the animal was dreaming of running, but then all movement stilled. That motion stopped the duo as they approached but now walked forward again. Extending the barrel of his rifle, Caleb poked the animal in the stomach, received no response and continued to the other downed buffalo. Repeating his action of before, he was assured both animals were down for the count.

"Well, good shootin' girl! That's your first buffalo, ain't it?"

With a nod of assent and a smile toward her partner, she said, "Sure is, an' I think he's bigger'n yours!"

"There ya go agin', always tryin' to show me up. If you

recall, I was a gentleman and let you have that one. So, you didn't get it cuz you're a better hunter, I gave it to you," he said grinning. "But, we need ta' get started butcherin' so let's start on your'n an' then we'll do the other'n."

With his razor sharp Bowie knife, Caleb split the bull from brisket to tail and started the butchering. After dragging out the guts and separating the liver and heart, the pair started the arduous process of stripping the skin to preserve the hide for the durable leather it would become. After cutting the hide into two smaller pieces, the meat was deboned and piled on the two pieces of hide and covered to protect from the hot sun. With no nearby trees, they hurried their labors and made short work of the repeated process on the second bull. While pulling the hide swathed bundles together, Caleb caught movement at the edge of the knoll as three men on horseback appeared and slowly made their way toward the two hunters. Caleb quickly spoke to Clancy, "Get your rifle and ready it, but stand easy."

His weapon was resting on the previously wrapped bundle nearby and Caleb casually strolled over to pick it up. As the three men approached, they greeted the hunters with, "Halloo there, mind if we come near?"

"Come ahead on if you're friendly," instructed Caleb.

As they approached, Caleb pulled the hammer back on the Hawken and lifted the barrel slightly though still holding it across his body. Clancy back-stepped nearer Caleb and held her rifle in the same manner. Two Bits moved to the side of his mistress and stood watchful. The larger of the three led the way and stopped his mount about fifteen yards from the site of the kill, looking at the remaining carcasses.

"Looks like you two got you a couple nice buffler. We been lookin' for some our own selves, but ain't found 'em yet," said Colby Jefferson as he looked at the two.

"The rest of the herd took off downstream when we got these two. They're probably grazing along the stream a bit farther down," replied Caleb with an unspoken suggestion for them to follow the herd.

"Well, it's gettin' too close to dark to do anymore huntin' anyway. Our camp's just a little ways back upstream thar if you wanna join us and maybe spend the night there," suggested Colby. "It's just me'n my brother, Cormick, and our partner, Miguel Martinez. We was part of a wagon train till our folks took sick. We buried 'em up yonder. Now we're just tryin' to stock up on meat n' such 'fore we head out to Fort Bridger to catch up with our wagon train," shared the larger youth, apparently the leader of the group.

"Well, we gotta get on back to our camp. The rest of our bunch is meetin' us back there and we're headin' to summer grounds with the village. So, thank ye for the invite, but we need to skedaddle," replied Caleb adding weight to his remark by mentioning the village.

"Village? What kinda village you talkin' 'bout? Is it someplace we can get supplies?" asked Cormick, the younger brother of the pair.

"No, it's an Arapaho village. We're on the move to our summer grounds."

"You mean you live with Injuns? I ain't never heard such a thing," commented Colby.

Clancy made a slow step closer to Caleb but watched the visitors with suspicion. The one at the rear, the Mexican, kept looking her over like a mountain lion looking for his next meal, and it was making her very uncomfortable. She had never experienced the look of lust before and this brought a touch of fear to her spirit.

"My pa was raised by 'em and we just live near 'em cuz they're friends. What you need to be concerned about is this country has more'n its share of other Indians. This area here is kinda the common spot for the Southern Ute that live South of here, the Cheyenne that are East of here and the Crow that are North of here. Course that's not to mention the Arapaho that we travel with," informed Caleb.

The three men looked at each other and with a nod from the leader, they reined their horses to the side and Colby said, "Well, we're headin' on back to camp. Good meetin' you, even though we didn't get your names."

"Hold on," said Caleb. He reached through a fold of the bundle at his feet and extracted a sizeable chunk of meat and handed it to the younger brother, now beside him. "Enjoy, and keep your top-knot on."

"Huh?"

"Keep your top-knot on. That means watch yourself and make sure some unfriendly Indian doesn't come along and scalp you. They do that, you know."

All three looked at Caleb with a surprised look showing, then at each other as they kneed their horses on their way. As the two hunters watched their visitors depart, Caleb turned to Clancy and said, "Let's get loaded and get outta here. I don't like the looks of them."

CAUTION BADE THEM MOVE THE CAMP TO A new location deeper in the canyon of the Popo Agie. The nights were still cold this early in Spring and in the depth of the canyon but there was still the threat of predators smelling fresh meat. Taking the necessary precaution, the two hunters hoisted the bundles of fresh buffalo meat high on the large limbs of the huge cottonwood beside the swift running creek. A cook fire just large enough for the small coffee pot and the overhanging strips of fresh meat was nestled in the ring of stones at the edge of the grass. The horses and mules were tethered downstream in a separate grove of cottonwood surrounded by thick willows, well protected and free to graze the plentiful greens. Using the packs and their saddles as back rests, Caleb and Clancy sought respite from the strenuous day and anticipated the fresh steaks now dripping juices into the cook fire.

"That was scary today," started Clancy.

"What do you mean?" asked Caleb uncertainly.

"Those three that came up on us at the kill, they were dirty and disgusting. That other one, the one in black, he kept looking at me. He made me think of a lion or a wolf that looks at their next meal."

"So, that's one time you didn't like some guy looking at you?" kidded her companion.

She looked sternly at him, then remembered the conversation from the previous night and his thoughts of other men looking at her. Smiling as she remembered his jealousy, she asked, "Were you jealous?"

"How could I be? I was too busy watching the other two. Sure they looked at you, but they acted like they didn't want to take their eyes off me. For a while there I thought they wanted to jump us and take our meat and everything."

"What would you have done if they tried?"

"Shot 'em."

"But you only had one shot with your rifle," she asked as a question.

"I still have Pa's Paterson colt in my belt. It's got five shots and that'd be more'n enough."

"You'd really protect me like that?" she asked leaning towards him and touching shoulders.

"You? I was protecting the meat! We worked hard for that buffalo and I was getting' hungry!" he said with a vain attempt at keeping a straight face that soon yielded to a broad smile.

Hitting him on the shoulder with a firm rap, she said, "You men are all alike!"

With a chuckle, he leaned forward for their coffee cups and reaching for the handle on the coffee pot, he poured the steaming brown liquid into the tin cups. Still smiling, he handed her the peace offering. She stretched out and grasped two of the willow branches that held strips of meat over the fire and brought them back to the common wooden plate between them. He started to grab one, but she slapped his hand and said, "You're supposed to say the prayer like Pa does, remember?"

Morning saw them starting early up the trail of Sinks Canyon. This was Clancy's first time on this part of the trail as the previous trips to the cabin followed the higher trail from the North. Caleb watched her face as they neared the cliff and boulders that obscured the mysterious rise of the sinks of the Popo Agie creek.

"Wait a minute," she said looking around, "where's the creek? It was just right here." She continued to scan the canyon bottom from side to side, then turning around at the sound of the cascading waters, she saw the stream beyond the boulders. It seemed to appear from underground and she turned her mount back for a closer look. As she neared the bubbling pool, she looked at Caleb and asked, "Did you know about this? It just comes up from nowhere!" Her head swiveled from Caleb to the water and back again watching him sit astride his mount with his hands on the saddle horn as he chuckled at her confusion.

"Come here, let me show you something." He turned his mount and headed up the trail leading the pack mule. Looking back at her as she took a last look at the pool, he said, "Come on."

A few moments later and farther up the trail, she once again heard the chuckling of cascading waters and saw at the South side of the canyon more greenery that revealed the presence of a stream. Caleb stopped the small cavalcade and dismounted motioning her to join him. After tethering their animals at a cluster of kinnikin-nick, he motioned for her to follow. A few steps brought them to the edge of the rushing stream that told of the increasing snow melt higher up the mountain. As it neared the cliff, it paralleled the wall then seemed to disappear into the face of the cliff. From the movement of the water, it was evident the stream went under an over-hang, but where it disappeared to, Clancy could not tell. She looked at Caleb with wonder written on her face and said, "It comes up way down there?" she motioned with her arm toward the lower canyon.

"Apparently, though some think these are two different streams entirely. No one really knows. Pa and I once threw a log in here," he motioned to the drop of the sinks, ". . . and we rode down there and waited for it to come out, but it never did. So, nobody really knows," he concluded with a shrug of his shoulders. He then turned to walk back to the horses and Clancy followed close behind. Now silent but wondering, she shook her head as she mounted up and took the lead rope of the mule. It would be closer to dusk when they made the cabin, but the eager travelers spurred their mounts back to the trail, anxiously wondering if Jeremiah and Waters would be waiting.

"When's that meat gonna be ready?" shouted Colby to his younger brother, Cormick.

"Hold your horses, it's almost ready," answered his brother.

"Ah, you Americanos, you're always een a hurry," added Miguel. The Mexican was leaning back against his saddle with his feet outstretched toward the fire. Cradling a warm cup of coffee in his hands, he added, "I weesh my momma was still here. At least she could cook a good meal."

"Yeah well, if you don't like it, fix your own," retorted the appointed cook, Cormick.

Colby walked closer to the fire before he dropped to a seat astraddle of his grounded saddle. Looking at the dripping meat that hung from the steel rod suspended over the fire, he thought of the many trappings fashioned by his father, a sometimes blacksmith. The rod over the fire was suspended on two Y shaped steel rods driven into the ground on either side of the fire. The same rod easily held the cast iron pots and Dutch ovens often used by their mother. There was also tripod of steel rods that held a flat plate for a frying pan or even a coffee pot. These, of course, were much too cumbersome to pack on horseback, but with the wagon for transport, this and the many other objects accumulated by the couple could easily be carried. But with four graves at the edge of the clearing, there was no one to give direction or guidance to the three young men.

As the hungry men partook of the fresh strip steaks, they were heedless of the juices dripping on their stain encrusted Linsey Woolsey shirts. Wiping their greasy fingers on their trousers, they refrained from conversation as they gorged themselves of the feast. Letting a loud belch sound forth into the surrounding trees and brush, Colby waited for an echo that never came. He had discovered a hidden jug of whiskey stored under the seat of the wagon and he now brought it to his lips, resting the weight of it on his extended elbow. Dropping it to his side, he yielded to his brother's demand for a share. The jug was passed to Miguel who immediately upped it to his lips and gulped several swallows before lowering it to take a deep breath.

Cormick opened the conversation with a statement, "I was lookin' at the supplies we got left, and it ain't much. We got enough powder and lead to last a while, unless some of them injuns show up, but everything else is gettin' mighty low."

"Whattaya want me to do about it?" countered Colby as he looked from Cormick to Miguel.

"Mebbee we should start out for that Fort Bridger the others spoke about," said Miguel in his sing-song accent.

"Well, I ain't in no hurry to catch up with that bunch of religious nuts. I had enough of them already, what with their Bible spoutin' and everthin'" grumbled Colby.

"We don't need ta catch up with 'em, but we are gonna need some supplies and that's the only place to be gettin' any!" affirmed Cormick.

"Now, let's don't go gettin' in such an all-fired hurry. We got 'nuff supplies for a while yet, and we could do some more huntin' for some meat. We could smoke some meat and such like we saw them pilgrims doin' and then when we got all we want, we can head out. Why, we might even join up with another wagon train."

"Yeah, maybe we can find a bigger one that's got more people and maybe some girls, too," said Cormick hopefully.

"Si, if we're lucky we find one with some senoritas that know how to treat a real man," sneered Miguel.

"I'm thinkin' I might like to get us that redhead we saw today. She looked like she was chained lightnin'" remarked Colby as a grin showed his brown teeth.

"No senor, those red heads are dangerous. That one looked ready to cut our hearts out, and that big dog, he was like a bear with his teeth showing. No, that one is trouble," warned the Mexican.

THE CAVALCADE OF DUSTY AND WEARY MOVERS arrived with a collective sigh of relief that rippled the waters of the small mountain lake that would be their source of water for the coming summer months. Across the water could be seen the black skeletons of the fire that destroyed so much of the timber and the camp of Black Kettle's village just two summers past. This would be the third summer since that tragedy, but the reminders stood stark and black with the spring growth of bushes and grasses in bright green giving renewed hope.

The week long travel had taken its toll on the many members of the Arapaho village, but the few remaining hours of daylight demanded another effort from the tired families. Lodges must be raised, horse herds taken to pasture and, of course, the evening meal must be prepared. Laughing Waters joined Pine Leaf as the two women set to the task of raising the lodge of Broken Shield and Pine Leaf. The experienced hands made short work of erecting the buffalo hide lodge and Leaf invited Waters and her family to stay with them for the meal.

Waters politely declined and Jeremiah was reminded of the polite society of the white man's world where the pinky-lifting fancy dressed women would have acted no differently than these two women of the mountains. Jeremiah turned to scoop up his young son and sat him on the saddle of the steel-dust then mounted behind him. Turning to Waters he said, "You comin' woman? We wanna make it to the cabin before it gets so dark we'll lose our way." She returned his smile with one of her own and mounted the strawberry roan to join her man. Reaching down to pat the horse on his neck, she purred, "Let's go Red, the old man's gettin' homesick again." She dug her heels into the roan's side and led the way to the trail that would take them home. Riding the gelding that was Caleb's first horse, she also led the blue roan that pulled the travois loaded with their many belongings. Jeremiah also led a pack horse and followed Waters into the thick timber and on the trail leading to their cabin.

Breaking into the clearing the welcome sight of the cabin stirred both Jeremiah and Waters with many pleasant memories. Both were surprised to see smoke coming from the chimney and they quickly looked to the nearby corral and saw the two mules and two appaloosas that told of Caleb and Clancy's presence. Pausing before the front door, Waters stepped down and handed the reins of her mount to Jeremiah, put Little John on her hip, then moved to the door.

She turned to look at her man before pushing the door open to surprise the young people inside. Looking through the open door, Jeremiah noted Caleb sitting at the table while Clancy was busy at the fire that held a suspended pot on the swinging metal arm. He smiled and gigged his horse while leading the three other animals to the corral.

Seeing his mother push the door open, Caleb smiled and said, "Hi Ma! You're just in time, Clancy's whippin' up a good meal for all of us. We weren't sure you would make it today or when, but here you are!"

Putting Little John down and watching as he toddled to Two Bits and dropped to rub his face in the belly of the big dog, she answered, "Yes, here we are, so how about you going out to help your father with the horses? And I'll help Clancy in here," she said after she hugged the son that was now much bigger than her. As he headed for the door she gave him a playful kick with her moccasin toe and turned to give Clancy a big hug as well. "So, how's my big girl, the mighty hunter? I see you brought the boy back safe. Did you get anything?"

"Sure did," replied Clancy, "we got a couple nice young bulls. The meat's hangin' high for tonight. We thought we'd start smokin' it tomorrow. We just had time to get it hung up before it started gettin' dark, so we came in to start supper."

Standing beside Clancy and with an arm lying across her shoulders, Waters watched as Clancy stirred the meat goulash in the swinging cast iron pot. Taking a deep breath, she turned toward the girl and asked, "So, did the two of you get anything talked out? You know, about what you were concerned about?"

Rapping the spoon on the side of the big pot, Clancy

turned to Waters and took a deep breath as well, then started, "Yeah, I think so. We pretty well agreed that we wanted to be together whatever the future brought for us," then smiling, she continued, "Whenever he talked about things he always used 'us' and 'we' and that made me feel good about it. But we just don't know for sure what that future is going to be, whether we stay here or go somewhere else or . . ." She let the thought hang without concluding, and turned back to the spoon and pot.

Waters moved to the counter and busied herself while she thought. She saw the remains in the bowl from the mixing of the corn meal and with a glance at the fire noticed the Dutch oven sitting at the side on some coals with other coals on the lid. She thought, *Clancy's got our meal well together and prepared. She will make a good woman and wife for the boy, if they could only get their minds together with their hearts*. Turning back to Clancy she said, "No one really knows what their future will be, there is so little we can do to make it what we will. But it is a good thing to know who it will be with. When I was your age, I thought much the same as you do now, and when Jeremiah was leaving to do what his father asked him to do, I was afraid I might never see him again. I did not know what my future would be and I did not know for sure who it would be with, but I made him promise to come back to me and he did."

After the initial greeting, the two men worked together silently as they removed the travois, the tack and the packs from the horses. Before putting the four mounts in the corral with the others, the men rubbed them down and brushed them out. The horses had worked long and hard and deserved the reward of a little pampering. Jeremiah noted the appearance of the mules and the appaloosas and could easily tell his son had taken care of them properly as well.

Leaning the long ends of the travois on the top rail of the corral fence, Jeremiah said, "I think we'll just leave that here for now and take care of it tomorrow. But after we put the tack away, let's get these packs into the house." Without comment, Caleb moved to carry out his father's instructions. The two men were loaded down with the packs, parfleches and saddle bags as they stepped into the cabin door. Greeted by the aroma of the meal, Jeremiah smiled and said, "Well girls, I see you've been busy. Sure smells good!" Clancy turned with a smile and stepped to give her Pa a kiss on the cheek as he stood with arms full of gear. Dropping the packs and gear against the wall by the door, the two men pulled out a chair from the table and seated themselves as if they had just finished a hard day's work.

Waters looked at the two and putting her hands on her hips she said, "Well, you two act like you were the only ones to do any work, when we women did just as much and more, as usual. But we are not sitting down and saying 'wait on me.'"

The two men looked at each other, then at the women, and started to stand but were pushed back down by a laughing Clancy and Waters. Bringing the pot to the table after putting the corn bread on a plate, the women joined the men for the evening meal. With the usual chit chat during the meal, the conversation focused on the hunt and the unwelcome visitors. With a concerned look that furrowed his brow, Jeremiah asked, "Did you find out much about them?"

"Not much. They said they had been with a wagon train that left 'em and then they buried their folks that had been sick with the Cholera. I figgered that's why the train left 'em behind. They said they were gonna stock up on meat and head out to Fort Bridger to re-supply and maybe catch up with another train," replied Caleb.

"They were dirty and I didn't like the looks of 'em either," interjected Clancy as she shook her shoulders in a shiver of disgust.

"Did you see which way they went and how far?" asked Jeremiah.

"They went farther up the valley, said they were camped by that little creek up there. We watched until they were outta sight, looked like they were arguin' 'bout sumpin."

"Well, hopefully you've seen the last of them. Did you have any other problems?"

"Nah, we had a good trip overall. Say, how's Grandfather doing? When we left, he was feelin' a little outta sorts," questioned Caleb with a concerned look shadowing his face.

Waters took that as her que to jump in the conversation with, "He's up and down, one day he acts like he's still a young man of twenty summers, and the next he acts like he's ready to cross over and be with our ancestors. He's asked about you and would be glad to see you."

"I want to see him too. Before we left he spoke of a vision quest and that's kinda got my interest up. That might be what I need to get goin' in the right direction," responded Caleb.

Clancy looked at him with a quizzical expression and wondered what was going on in his mind that he needed direction. She was certain they had agreed on the direction they were going. Maybe she was assuming too much and maybe he was still confused. *If he keeps that up, I'm going to be just as confused as ever. Did I do something wrong? What happened to the 'we' and 'us' he was talking about before?*

"I think I'll go see him tomorrow after we get everything settled in here. I'd like to know more about the vision quest. He said most young men of the people would go on one, but that it wasn't a requirement or anything, just a searching of yourself and your life. Is that right, Ma?" Caleb looked to his Ma for an answer.

She looked at her son, then replied, "Well, my son, that is what I understand it to be. I did not go on one though I could have if I wanted to, but I did not need any answers. I knew what I wanted and who I wanted to be with, but many young men do go on a quest, even if they have direction to their life. It is really a spiritual thing to draw closer to the Great Spirit, or in your case, to your God."

"I guess I'm like that too. I know who I want to be with," he said as he looked at Clancy now with her head bowed and looking at the floor, but that comment caused her to look up and into the eyes of Caleb, "but it was more of a thing for me to know more about myself and my God. Grandfather said it could be good for me as I become a man and a warrior. But I think it would also be something special for me and him together. He once said He might go with me."

Waters was surprised at this because a vision quest was usually something sought at the beginning of adulthood, but her father was a leader of the people and a respected Shaman. She couldn't understand why he would go on a vision quest, unless it was actually something else. The look of consternation crossed her face, though she tried to hide it from the others. *What is he thinking to make a quest like this, and what else could it be? Maybe it's some special ritual or rite or ceremony for a Shaman. But if I am to become the Shaman, shouldn't I know of this? I must ask him soon.*

THE SUN HAD YET TO CRAWL ABOVE THE treetops but every member of the family was busy with the many tasks of settling in for the summer. Waters and Clancy returned from a cluster of willows with an armload of branches for the drying racks as Caleb and Jeremiah lowered the bundles of buffalo meat down from the elevated perches.

Scratch was disappearing up the trail to the higher meadow leading the many animals on a string. The rawhide rope used to tie tail to halter for the string of animals to be led single file, was a braided and durable rope with many uses around the cabin. Little John and Two Bits were happily playing in the lone sunny spot on the West edge of the clearing. Seating themselves at the edge of the sunshine, Waters and Clancy began the task of assembling the drying and smoking racks for buffalo.

The large cuts of meat would be cut into long and thin strips, hung on a rack suspended over a low and slow burning fire that would be fed with damp wood for smoking. The meat would be preserved and could be stored for months if necessary. After the preparation of the meat, the women would busy themselves scraping the hides and start the curing or tanning of the hides to be used as robes or the many other uses for the leather such as lodges and moccasins.

The men busied themselves with the packs, the animals, and work on the storage cave, the corrals and buildings and the many pieces of tack and gear that demanded repair and maintenance.

As Caleb and his Pa were sorting the many items contained in the packs, Jeremiah turned to the lad and said, "So, you think you've got things figured out about you and Clancy?"

"I think so, but it's not just me an' her bein' together, but what're we gonna do? You know, where we're gonna live and stuff like that."

"What about just stayin' here and bein' part of the family?" asked Jeremiah.

"You know how it is Pa, we want our own life. We talked a little about stayin' here an all, but we're just not sure. We even talked a little about goin' back to the white man's world, the city an' all that, but neither of us really want that."

"Is that what's got you thinkin' about a vision quest?"

"Maybe, well, sorta, yes. But I also want to spend some time with Grandfather. He said he has a lot to teach me, or like he said, guide me into. He said a quest would be good for me and could help me in my life. How it'll do that, I don't know, but I thought I would talk to him about it anyway," surmised Caleb as he continued his work with the packs.

"Son, I wish I could tell you what your life is supposed to be cuz I kinda know what you're goin' through. I was about your age when Ezekiel was killed and Shield, Waters and I set out to get the ones that done it and make that long trip back to Kentucky. It seemed like all the way there I was questioning what my life was goin' to be and such, but I kept thinkin' 'bout Waters, cuz she had to bring Shield back to the village. And I kept wonderin' if we were sposed to be together and the more I thought about it, the more I realized I couldn't picture my life without her in it. But it's more than just who you're gonna be with, it's what you're gonna do with your life. Now, me, I found a place here with family, you know, you and Clancy and now Little John, and with Water's people. And we're happy, I can see us livin' out our days right here in the tall timber. But, of course, that's not for everyone."

Caleb looked at his Pa and smiled with a shake of his head and said, "Pa, I ain't never heard you talk that much at one time, ever! But thanks for that. It's good to know I ain't the only one goin' through this."

"I'm sure you'll get it all figured out in due time, Son. And even if you don't, life has a way of workin' things out for us, especially when we trust the Lord to guide us."

Scratch had returned from the upper meadow and now led the way as the family gravitated to the cabin for the mid-day meal. The sun hung high in the clear blue sky and the clearing held two smoke fires with meat basking in the grey clouds that circled their way heavenward. Staked at the edge of the clearing were four pieces of buffalo hide. Each hide had been split to provide the covering for the bundles of meat and to make the packs balanced for the pack mules. The women had made short work of the scraping and cleaning of the hides but much work remained to cure the hides and make them into soft and pliable leather.

As the family entered the cabin, Waters said, "We've got enough of last night's fixin's and corn bread for a quick meal. If that is not enough, there is also some pemmican left from our move." Turning to Caleb she asked, "Do you still want to see Grandfather?"

"Yeah, I thought if we were caught up enough, I might go up there today," replied Caleb.

"We will go together. I want to talk to him too," she said without explanation. A nod of the head from Caleb was enough of an answer and she padded past the men to ready the meal.

Two Bits led the way through the pine forest as the small group followed on the familiar trail. Clancy had decided to join Caleb and Ma on the return visit to the village. Little John sat in front of Clancy as the two shared the seat of the saddle and the youngster was busy with his jabbering and pointing at the many wonders of the world around him. He would look at the bird landing on a tree branch and point and tell Clancy to "Look!"

When Caleb mimicked the song or call of a bird, the child would look first at the bird, then back at Caleb and again at the bird. After several times of this confusion, when Caleb mimicked the call of a dove, Little John scowled at Caleb and said, "No," as if to direct his brother to not make the sound. The laughter of the trio that accompanied him prompted the child to join in the fun and re-focused his attention to the trail ahead.

Arriving in the village, they went directly to the lodge of Black Kettle. Stopping in front of the lodge and starting to dismount, they were greeted by the elder statesman with a cheery, "Ah, my family. It is good for you to visit me so soon. Come, sit with me and we will talk."

Caleb faced the Shaman and said, "Greetings, Grandfather."

A similar greeting was echoed by both Waters and Clancy as Clancy stood Little John before her. The child looked at the grey headed man with the weathered and wrinkled skin and smiled and said, "Ganfar," as he walked quickly to the old man and lifted his arms to be picked up. The Grandfather chuckled and gladly obliged the boy. He lifted Little John and sat him on his hip and smiled as he tickled the boy under the arms. Receiving a giggle and a squirm, Black Kettle turned to Waters and said, "Before you leave, be sure to see Pine Leaf. She was asking about you this morning and I think she has something to talk to you about."

"We will go there now. The One Who Talks to the Wind wants to visit with you. I will leave you two and Sun of the Morning will come with me to the lodge of my brother." Though Broken Shield was not her brother, he had been raised by Black Kettle as his own and Shield and Waters had referred to one another as brother and sister. Shield was the son of Black Kettle's brother, Buffalo Hump, who had been killed in battle when Shield was a babe. Shield's mother had died in childbirth and the only father he knew was Broken Shield. Pine Leaf had become the wife of Shield after Jeremiah and Shield had rescued her after a battle between the Crow and the Blackfeet. Pine Leaf had been a War Leader and Pipe Bearer of the Crow, but was wounded during the fight and almost died before Shield had taken her to his camp, bound up her wounds and helped her to recover. Shortly after, they were joined in a simple ceremony by the Crow chief. Now she lived with her mate, Broken Shield, in the village of the Arapaho.

"Greetings to the wife of my brother," spoke Waters as she approached the lodge of Broken Shield and Pine Leaf.

"And greetings to you, my friend. It is good to see you again so soon. I know it was a long time, what, oh yes, that was just one day ago," she giggled as she spoke. "Come into my lodge, I have something to tell you," she said with a mischievous smile tugging at the corners of her mouth.

Clancy told Two Bits to lay down beside the lodge, then ducking her head to enter with Little John at her hip, she followed Waters into the cooler lodge. Leaving the entrance flap folded back on the side of the dwelling to give more light, Leaf motioned for her company to be seated. As they lowered themselves to be seated on a stack of buffalo robes and blankets, Waters looked around the lodge and commented, "You have been busy. Your home looks like it has been here a long time, not just one day."

Pine Leaf could stay her excitement no longer as she sat down to face her friend and share the news. "I am going to have a baby!" And with that simple announcement, the women began to chatter like generations of women have done in lodges, homes, camps and any other place that women gathered. It would be some time before the excited chatter would subside and the women could part company.

"Grandfather, I came to talk to you about the vision quest you mentioned."

"Oh, are you thinking about doing a vision quest, my son?"

"Yes, I've been thinkin' about it quite a lot, really. I think it would be good for me to do one, at least as far as I know about it. Do you think I should?" asked Caleb, with an anxious look on his face.

"It has been on my heart as well. Maybe the Great Spirit is speaking to both of us. Yes, I think it would be a good thing for you to do. Have you spoken to your mother and father about this?" quizzed the Shaman.

"Some, I believe they think it's up to me. Can you tell me a little more about it?"

Seating himself more comfortably, the old man began, "When one begins a vision quest, it must start with prayer. Once you decide, then you must begin to pray to your God and then we start with other preparations. First, you must make a pipe, as a pipe is very important. It is a symbol of what you are to be, firm yet empty, or hollow, so that the Spirit may speak to you. You must also gather the things we will need.

I will go with you as your Shaman and instruct you as

we go. It is not always so that the medicine man joins in the quest, but it is a good thing for one to have the medicine man with him so he does everything just right. Now, my son, you must understand this is a spiritual thing you will do and it is not to be done except with a pure heart. That is why you must begin your prayer and continue to pray all the while we make preparations.

The Spirit has led me to go to the great Medicine Wheel for this quest. It will be a journey of about seven suns to get to the Medicine Mountain. The vision quest will be perhaps two or three or even more days. This will be very challenging for you but also very rewarding. Do you believe you can do this?"

Caleb did not answer quickly but pondered all that Black Kettle had said. Lifting his head to his Grandfather, he answered, "Yes, I believe I can do this, Grandfather."

"Good. First you must prepare a pipe. I will give you a piece of soapstone, but you will have to find a good piece of alder or willow for the stem. Also you will need to make four small flags about half the size of an arrow, of four different colors. You will also need a blanket and breechcloth and supplies for the trip up and back. You must begin your prayer as soon as you leave here. I will come to you at your home at the end of two days. We will leave together the next morning." Black Kettle stood and as Caleb stood beside him, the old man grasped his forearm with his own and nodded his head in dismissal. Without another word, the Shaman entered his lodge to begin his own preparations.

Caleb walked behind the lodge, picked up the tethers

of the three mounts and started through the village in search of Waters and Clancy. Within a few moments, he arrived at the lodge occupied by the gabby women and little boy. Since Water's arrival, two other women had joined the excited group and the chattering had continued unabated. As another woman started to enter, Caleb implored her to tell Waters and Clancy he was waiting. After spending another quarter hour waiting, he was finally rewarded with their presence as they exited the lodge with broad smiles and laughter that followed them from the dwelling.

The cheerful women mounted up and Caleb handed Little John to his mother, mounted and with Two Bits following, led the trio homeward.

"SO, MA, HAVE YOU EVER MADE A PIPE BEFORE?" asked Caleb as he examined the piece of soapstone he received from his Grandfather.

"No, but I've seen my father make them and if you want, I can help you," she said as she looked across the table at her son.

"I think I'm gonna need all the help I can get," he said softly as he turned the soapstone over and over in his hands.

"Is there something I can do to help?" asked Clancy with her chin in her hands and propped on her elbows on the table.

"Yeah, there is. I'm gonna need four small flags, half the size of an arrow. Red, White, Black and Yellow about the size of your hand. That'd be great, Clancy. Thanks."

"O.K. you get your father's tools, the drill and files and that will make this go a lot faster. Go on outside, because working with this stone is very dusty and I do not want it on my table," instructed Waters.

At Water's instruction, Caleb used the brace and bit with a small bit to start drilling the hole in the stem part of the stone. The bowl of the pipe was to be larger than the drills that Jeremiah had, so Waters showed Caleb how to use a flint tipped arrow. Placing the soapstone between his knees, then with the tip of the arrow resting at the beginning point for the bowl, he began to spin the arrow between his palms, back and forth, to start the drilling process. Often blowing the dust away, he slowly made progress with the hard flint and the soft stone. With the bowl and the stem hole joined, he began shaping and carving the exterior of the pipe. Caleb had decided on an eagle head for the base of the bowl and with the practiced fingers of an artisan, Water's carefully instructed the young man in the craft. Several hours had passed before the pipe began to resemble what Caleb had envisioned.

"Now, after you finish smoothing the stem and the bowl with the sandstone, you can take the sand in your hands and smooth it even more but it will be slow. After you are done, we will use water for an even smoother finish," instructed Waters.

Soapstone is basically very hard packed clay making it easy to shape and fashion with hard tools and careful hands. After the smoothing and the use of water to polish, the young man used the sharp tip of flint to enhance his design, making the appearance of feathers on the eagle and highlighting the eyes. The sandy red color of the stone had become a work of art. As he blew some air through the stem and sent a small cloud of dust from the bowl, Waters waved her hand in front of her face to clear the dust and frowned at her son.

"Whew . . . well, with that done, after we have something to eat, we'll work on the pipe stem. While I fix something to eat, you go get either a piece of Alder or ash that will be long and straight enough for a stem. And be sure to get it big enough to make it easier to carve down to size."

"O.K. Ma, thanks. Clancy, you wanna come with me?" he asked as he started for the lower end of the clearing and the nearby stream.

"Sure, I'll come. I saw some good wood that might work when I was getting your flag stems," she commented as she followed Caleb on the errand.

Letting Clancy take the lead, Caleb willingly followed her to the previously sighted wood. It was a pile of driftwood that had accumulated from the early spring runoff from the melting snow of the mountains. Sticking out of the pile was a piece of wood a bit longer than Caleb's forearm and about the same size around. It looked straight enough and although Caleb wasn't sure what kind of wood it was, he thought it would be just right for what he wanted. He climbed up the unsteady pile, latched on to the large stick and pulled it loose. The sudden momentum shift and the uncertain footing took its toll as Caleb fell backwards into the stream. Fortunately, it was shallow and he was able to stand to the accompaniment of laughter from Clancy. "Hey, you're s'posed to be gettin' wood, not goin' fishin'!"

Standing in the shallow water that was knee high to him, Caleb stood with the stick in one hand and pointed it at Clancy, "Don't just stand there, give me a hand!"

Clancy stepped to the edge of the bank and still

laughing stretched her hand out to the waterlogged Caleb. He tossed the small log to the bank and reached his hand for hers, grasped her wrist and pulled her into the water with him. As she screamed, they both ended up sitting in the shallow pool, side by side, and laughing at each other.

"Great, now what is Ma gonna say about us goin' swimmin' in the middle of the day?" she asked with the wide grin that matched Caleb's. Helping each other up, they trudged to the creek bank, stepped to the grassy area and sat down, still laughing. Clancy turned to Caleb and asked, "Is there something goin' on with you that you have to do this vision quest?"

"Well, yes and no. Really, between you and me, this is as much for Grandfather as it is for me. Oh, I want to do it, but it's just from a, well, a spiritual side of things. What with us talkin' about spendin' the rest of our lives together, I want to be the man you need me to be. Do you understand that?"

She stared at the young man at her side and was moved with a deep emotion at this revelation. He was not just thinking of himself, he was thinking about them and this was for their life together. Breathing deeply, she touched his hand and looked into his eyes saying, "Yes, I understand now. That means a lot to me. I like the thought of us spending our lives together. I don't think anything could make me happier." Looking at Caleb, then down at her wet buckskins, she said, "Well, maybe dryin' off would make me happy right now," then jumping up, she said, "Come one, pollywog, let's go get somethin' to eat!" As she ran toward the clearing, Caleb was close behind.

After the quick meal, the trio returned to the previous tasks. At Water's instructions, Caleb built a small fire in the fire ring away from the cabin. After the blaze was going, she had Caleb fetch the rifle cleaning rod and a long piece of heavy wire used for a handle on the Dutch oven. When he returned, she had him place the cleaning rod in the fire, then straightening the heavy wire, she placed the end of it in the fire also.

While they waited for the work of the fire, she had Caleb start by cutting the wood into a proper length using the bow saw from the tack shed. Then she put him to work whittling the bark from the wood and beginning the design on the pipe stem. By this time the iron rod and wire were both sufficiently hot and she instructed him to use the larger rod and start burning the draw hole in the center of the wood and most of the length of the wood. He had to switch ends and alternate using the wire on the mouth end and the rod on the pipe end, using one and heating the other. The alternating work soon saw the long draw hole connected within the interior of the long piece of wood.

"Good, now you can taper the bowl end to a size small enough to fit into the stem end of the bowl. When you complete that end, work on the end for the mouth-piece. Only after you get that done, do you work on the design on the length of the stem." She looked at him questioningly to see if he understood and with a nod of his head, she turned to go to the cabin. Motioning to Clancy to join her, the two disappeared into the dwelling.

The time of solitude and business gave Caleb an opportunity to occupy his mind with the prayer as instructed by his Grandfather. His hands moved with a rhythm as they carved and smoothed the pipe stem, and the monotonous rhythm allowed his mind to dwell on the coming quest and the inquiry of his heart regarding his future. Although not particularly worded, the thoughts of prayer moved through his mind as he considered what lay before him with the quest, the purpose of the journey, and his time with his Grandfather. Soon his thoughts turned to Clancy and the possible future together and what trails their lives would follow. *Possibilities, directions, maybes, but no answers, I guess that's what this quest will answer for me. At least I hope so.*

Holding the pipe stem at arm's length, he admired his handiwork. The handbreadth of length nearest the bowl was plain, but in the middle of the stem he had carved a spiral that gave the pipe-stem the look of a large screw, then the portion nearest the mouth piece had a simple carving of swirls and flowers. There was still some work to do to smooth it out and maybe some painting or other decoration, but he was happy with his work. He stood and stepped into the cabin to surprise the women as they were busy with beadwork and leatherwork on the table. Smiling at her son, Waters said, "Let me see what you have done," and held her hand out for the pipe. Turning it over in her hands, she then handed it to Clancy and said, "O.K. add the special part."

Taking a step closer to the table, Caleb said, "Wait, what do you mean 'add the special part'?"

"Just watch and see," replied his Ma with a broad smile.

Clancy then placed a piece of fringed buckskin and wrapped it around the pipe, securing it with a swipe of horse-hoof glue. She then wrapped a beaded design around the leather and bound it with a slender piece of rawhide, giving the pipe a bright decoration on the plain smooth section nearest the bowl. Then, attaching a strip of fringed rawhide to the bottom of the stem and letting the fringe dangle with a large colored bead at the end of each piece of fringe, the pipe was almost complete. All that remained was a coating of beeswax to both stem and bowl to preserve and add sheen to both wood and stone. Extending it to Caleb she said, "We have asked the Creator to use this to give you the guidance you seek."

Caleb looked into the eyes of Clancy and saw the love and sincerity and turning to his Ma, he realized that both these women held a special love and concern for him and his quest. *This is really going to be special and I know God is going to give me the direction I seek.*

THE LONG EARLY MORNING SHADOWS stretched across the trail that twisted its way through the black timber. The brisk air that hung amidst the ponderosa and stretched their long needled branches for first light penetrated the buckskin tunics worn by both Caleb and his Grandfather.

The long-legged appaloosa stallion that bore Caleb was happily stretching out on the trail and was dragging the unwilling pack mule behind. Followed by Grandfather on his favorite buffalo pony, an agile paint mustang that quick-stepped down the trail so as not to be left behind, Caleb shivered with the cold but knew warmth would soon come when the trail broke into the sunshine on the lower slope. Animals and man alike were glad to be on the way of the vision quest, animals, because it released them from the crowded meadows and corrals, and man because the long talked about quest was finally under way.

Just as the fullness of the golden orb was visible on

the far horizon, the travelers cleared the thick timber and were following the angled trail that would take them to the valley floor. Scattered Juniper and Pinion stood tall compared to the skeletal figures of the cholla cactus. The patches of prickly pear cactus fought for moisture with the scrubby blue green sage. Making their way through the red clay and tan sandstone valley, they followed the trail to the cut between the ridges that revealed the Wind River valley. The slow descending foothills soon yielded their prominence to the flatter and much greener lowlands. New sprouts of the buffalo grass and occasional patches of wheatgrass prompted the animals to drop their heads and grab a mouthful of the tempting treat without missing a step on their journey. Now in the flatlands, Grandfather moved up alongside his grandson to give directions for their route.

Lifting a bony finger to point toward the Northeast, he said, "Grandson, we will go in that direction, cross Beaver creek before it enters the Wind River, and continue toward those two mountains to a trail that is east of the shorter one." There was a continuous range of smaller mountains, foothills really, called the Owl Creek Mountains, that ran from the Needles of the Absaroka due east for two to three day's ride, then turned north and joined with the Bighorns.

The mountains Grandfather pointed to were the last mountains in the Owl Creek range before that range joined the Bighorns. These smaller mountains were not the towering crags usually thought of as the Rockies that held the winter snows on pointed peaks, but were more rugged. These were the mountains that truly fit the description of rocky with huge deposits of large boulders and rugged valleys, canyons, arroyos and mesas with rimrock and box canyons, hidden valleys and meadows.

Populated with mule deer, antelope and buffalo, these mountains were also the home of many of the Cheyenne, Crow, and even Sioux on the far Eastern slopes. Although the Arapaho were allies with the Cheyenne, and more recently a pact had been made with the Crow because of the mating of Broken Shield and Pine Leaf, the Sioux were still sworn enemies of the Arapaho. Yet it was through this territory that their journey would take them to the Bighorns and to the Medicine Wheel.

The undulating plains before them maintained a mysterious manner, first hiding then revealing some distant landmark. Before they bottomed out in the Wind River valley, Caleb had taken a sight on the distant greenery that marked the confluence of the Wind River and Beaver Creek, but that landmark was not always visible. With the rolling contours of the valley floor obscuring their view, Caleb found himself randomly identifying the many cactus, grasses and occasional flowers on their route. He leaned to the right side of his mount to get a closer look at an unusual cluster of budding purple flowers that he thought might be the purple coneflower that healers used for snakebite.

In that instant, a sound that Caleb first thought of as dry leaves blowing in the wind, was identified by his horse as a rattlesnake and Caleb tightened his grip on the saddle horn as his horse launched himself almost six feet straight in the air. It was only the swell of the pommel of the saddle that saved him from immediately sliding to the ground. Using his legs and every part of his body he could muster, Caleb grabbed for any handhold to keep himself from becoming airborne and landing either in the Rattlesnake's lap or the nearby patch of prickly pear cactus.

With every stiff-legged jump the appaloosa let out a snort and a squeal as he interpreted the contact of Caleb as a strike from the snake. Each jump seemed to launch the pair higher in the air and with another valiant drop and spring from coiled spring-like legs, the horse twisted in the middle with his front legs pointing West and the hind legs pointing East and the rider pointing in four different directions with the flopping limbs of his torso. As the airborne duo began another descent, the only contact Caleb had with the saddle was a weak grip on the horn as his feet were pointing heavenward and his face was furrowing the mane of the Appaloosa.

The sudden stop of the equine did not stop the rapid descent of his rider as Caleb found a landing spot free of cactus but not free of rocks. His crumpled form was twisted in an unorthodox manner and his face was lodged between two stones. He barely heard the snorting and squealing of his horse as it fled the scene.

"Grandson, grandson, speak to me. Grandson!"

The feeble voice seemed to come from far away and there was nothing but darkness. Realizing his nose was pressed against the dirt, Caleb exhaled and stirred the sandy soil into his eyes and open mouth. The reflexive jerk back from the eye irritant freed his face from the stones and caused him to reach for support with his hands with one landing smack on top of a new sprout of a nearby prickly pear cactus. Jerking back from that he slowly rolled to his side and squinted his dust-filled eyes to see where he was, but the voice of his grandfather assured him he was not alone. He pulled at his eyelids and sought to clear his vision and with the second attempt was successful. He looked around and said, "Where's my horse?"

"The last I saw of him, he was going north," indicated his Grandfather with an outstretched arm toward the distant cluster of cottonwood.

With every movement, Caleb was reminded of his brief adventure atop the Pegasus of the plains and wondered if he was going to have to walk all the way to the Medicine Wheel.

"I think we will find him by the river. I do not think he will go too far," stated the wise old patriarch. Caleb noticed the pack mule's lead rope was tethered to the saddle of his grandfather's mustang.

"Well, at least we didn't lose the mule. I guess I'll have to walk after that crazy spotted horse of mine, that is, if I can walk. I feel like I got buried under a rockslide."

"The rocks did not fall on you. You fell on the rocks. But I did get our supper," he said as he held up the headless rattlesnake.

Caleb looked at his grandfather, then at the snake and back at his grandfather and asked, "We're gonna eat that?"

Shaking his head in the affirmative, he responded, "Tastes just like prairie chicken!"

Struggling to get up and stretch his legs, Caleb examined his limbs and torso for any wounds but found nothing but a few scrapes and several sore spots that would bring color in the days ahead. He went to the side of the mustang and untied the lead rope of the mule and motioning to his Grandfather, started following the tracks of his wayward mount. True to Grandfather's prediction, the horse was on a straight-line course to the river and the trail taken was an easy one to follow. The travelers had not stopped since morning but continued on the trek after the appaloosa. After the first couple of miles, Caleb had worked out his soreness and moved at a pace that equaled the short strides of the mustang.

"Grandson, you did a fine job on that pipe. Have you also been keeping your thoughts in prayer like I said?"

"Mostly grandfather, but I'm not used to doing that, so sometimes my mind wanders to other things. But then I think those other things should also be a matter of prayer, you know, like when I get to thinkin' about me and Clancy and our future together," commented the young man as he looked up at his elder. "Am I right, shouldn't that be part of my prayer?"

"Yes, you are right. Everything about your life should be a part of your prayer. But this is just the beginning of your quest. The journey is to make you focus on your prayer and your life. There will be many things that will test you, like the snake and your walk. Sometimes these are from the evil of the world to keep you from your quest, and sometimes these things will be allowed by the Great Spirit or your God to help you understand how important this time is for you."

As he walked, Caleb thought about what his Grandfather said, and turning these things over in his mind he considered each one carefully. *Hmmm . . . my mom used to talk about the way Satan worked. I didn't think it meant anything, but there really is evil in this world. I never thought of it like that. But Pa says God is bigger than anything! I guess that means He's bigger than any of the evil in the world too. That's good to know. O.K. God, I've been prayin' and talkin' to you a lot lately, and like Grandfather says, this journey is for you and me to get closer, so that's what I'm askin' for, for you and me to be closer and understand each other better. Course, I guess you already understand me, so it's me that's gotta understand you better.*

"There's your horse," stated his Grandfather as he pointed to the cluster of willows at the bank of Beaver creek. As he spoke, the appaloosa lifted his head to take in the visitors to his grassy banquet and with a look that said, "Where ya been?" he watched as Caleb and company joined him by the shallow stream.

"This will be a good place to camp. We can have fresh meat for our meal," said his Grandfather as he slipped from his mount. Caleb had successfully retrieved his mount and now took the reins of the mustang and the lead rope from the mule to tether the animals in for the night. Once they were tied off, he removed the tack from the saddle horses then dropped the packs from the mule. Dragging the gear to a common pile on a grassy area by the trees, he then made a fire circle and started the cook fire for the night. Grandfather was busy preparing the snake and surprised Caleb when he presented several filets of white meat to be cooked in the small skillet that was warming next to the coffee pot.

With the meal done and gear put away, Caleb admitted to his Grandfather that the rattlesnake really did taste like prairie chicken, or as some would say, sage grouse. With the bedrolls stretched out on the grassy knoll to afford a comfortable cushion for the night, the chuckle of the nearby stream providing a comforting distraction from Caleb's bruises and scrapes, both grandson and grandfather anticipated a good night's rest. There was no conversation as both men slipped into their individual reveries and stared at the multitude of stars that decorated the night sky. The Milky Way arched over the campers as the night time rainbow offered ample assurance of the presence of the Creator.

A LOW MONOTONE ʀᴜᴍʙʟᴇᴅ ɪɴᴛᴏ Cᴀʟᴇʙ's consciousness and stirred him awake. The chuckle of the nearby stream had lulled his senses and allowed a restful night, but the monotone hum came from beyond the cluster of trees and past the tethered animals. Looking at the unoccupied bedroll, Caleb realized what he heard was the chanting prayer of his Grandfather.

Feeling a little guilty about his late arousal, he rolled from his comfortable bed and walked to the edge of the trees to mimic the prayer time he often witnessed by his father. Finding a prone log big enough for a seat, he faced the rising sun and pondered his actions and his quest. His conversation with God was simple and silent as he allowed his thoughts to turn to the possibilities of his future. Then with a simple, "It's all in your hands, God," he rose to return to the fire ring and his responsibilities of preparing the animals for the journey.

With the mule packed, Caleb started to rig up his horse with bridle and saddle, saddle bags and parfleche, rifle and scabbard. Grandfather joined him and was saddling his mount as he asked his grandson, "Did you start your day with prayer, grandson?"

"Yes, Grandfather, I just don't have as many things to pray about as you do, I guess," he said with a smile as he looked over the saddle at his grandfather.

"That's because I have so many things to thank the Creator for, I have had a long life."

"I thought our prayin' was supposed to be more about askin' than thankin'," replied the youngster.

"That is the problem with you, young people, you never say thank you enough," stated the old man with a grin at the youth. "May be that is why the Creator gave you those two black eyes to remind you to be thankful."

"What? What'dya mean, black eyes?" said a startled Caleb as he reached up to feel his face and noticed a slight swelling below his eyes. "Are you tellin' me, I've got black eyes?"

"There is a still pool of water beyond that tree, go see your black eyes."

Trotting to the edge of the stream and the still back-water pool, the young man flopped down on his belly and suspended his face over the pool to see his reflection. From his eyebrows down to about even with the end of his nose, it appeared as one big purple and blue bruise spread across his face. The swelling was just beginning to puff out his cheeks but promised to do more. He also noticed that his face wasn't the only tender spot on his body as he pushed up from the edge of the stream. A sore elbow, the heels of both hands, both knees and part of his lower chest were reminders of his short flight of the previous day. Emitting a growling groan, he walked back to the horses and his grandfather.

"I didn't think I felt too bad, until I saw what I looked like. Then it seems like I began to hurt all over. This is gonna be a long trip," he grumbled as he returned to the side of his mount and finished cinching the saddle down tight.

"But grandson, sometimes the journeys we remember the most are the shortest ones. Like the short journey you took from the back of your horse to the ground," chuckled his grandfather.

By mid-afternoon they'd covered a considerable distance across the easy traveling plains. The terrain varied little from the rolling hills, occasional low flat-top plateaus with rim rock and the ever-present sandstone slabs and sagebrush. They passed a sizeable herd of buffalo that was slowly grazing its way to the river bottom and kicked up plenty of jack rabbits. The antelope were plentiful and scattered across the plains in small herds and even many individual bucks.

With little thought of taking game, the duo enjoyed the trek across the arid plains. Because of the rolling terrain and enemy territory, they traveled through the swales, valleys and gulches to prevent sky-lining themselves before anyone with hostile intent. Yet with all their caution, as they rounded a bend in the gulley that cut through a fold between two overshadowing mesas, their way was blocked by a line of six mounted warriors. The immediate threat caused Caleb to reach for his Hawken riding in the scabbard under his right leg, but the hand of Black Kettle on his arm stayed his defensive action. As he looked to his Grandfather, he caught a glimpse of another line of warriors that had moved to block the ravine behind them. With a nod of his head and a simple, "Uhhh . . ." he told his Grandfather of the additional threat.

Grandfather looked to the group in front of them and called out, "Snake Eater, is that you? Why are you not back in your lodge with your woman and your many little ones? He spoke in the Arapaho tongue, but lapsed into the tongue of the visitors.

Snake Eater? Did he just call him Snake Eater? After what we had last night? thought Caleb.

"Black Kettle? You should be back in the mountains where you belong. I heard you had crossed over to visit your ancestors, but I see it is not so. Who is this white pup you ride with?"

Caleb did not understand the dialect used by the two apparently acquainted warriors. But the looks, laughter and gestures told Caleb he was the object of their discussion.

"This is my grandson. We are going to the Medicine Wheel for a vision quest. Tell me, is your father Yellow Wolf still as ugly as ever?" This remark drew laughter from the other warriors as their chief, Yellow Wolf was known for his fierce countenance even when happy.

"I cannot speak of my father but I know he would have you come to our village for a meal and a visit. You and the little raccoon will come with us to see your old friend?" asked the leader of the hunting party. They were from the *He´vhaitanio* band of the Southern Cheyenne.

They were commonly known as the *Hair Rope Men* because of their reputation as the best horse tamers and horse raiders from the surrounding tribes. Led by Yellow Wolf and Big Man, this band of Southern Cheyenne had long been allies of the Arapaho, and Yellow Wolf and Black Kettle were long-time friends. The "wolf cub" and his grandfather willingly followed the hunting party to their village that lay in a long narrow and green valley watered by a small spring- fed creek. The group that served as their escort were part of the Bowstring society, similar to the well-known dog soldiers, they were a select group of warriors charged with the protection of the village. Although the Southern Cheyenne were part of the Treaty of 1825 negotiated by General Henry Atkinson and Indian Agent Benjamin O'Fallon, there were still conflicts with the Sioux and other warring tribes that were not part of that treaty.

Upon their arrival to the village, the many women and children flocked to the returning warriors and were surprised at the visitors. Some recognized Black Kettle as an old ally and friend and shouted their welcome. Still Caleb was unable to understand the language, but he was cognizant of the attitudes and welcome offered by the people. As they stopped in front of a prominent lodge, Snake Eater instructed them to dismount and wait for the chief, Yellow Wolf. Within moments, a tall and broad shouldered though wrinkled and aged warrior exited the lodge and with a broad smile extended his arms to welcome his old friend.

"Black Kettle, my friend. It has been many summers since we have fought together. Come, sit, we will eat and talk of old times and the many coups we have counted."

"Yellow Wolf, it is so good to see you, my old friend.

How have you managed to last these many summers, and where are your women and your children? Are you still the one known as "chief plenty pups" because of your crowded lodge?" kidded his old friend. It was evident these two were old and dear friends.

The camaraderie shared by them was contagious as many of the band crowded around to enjoy the friendship and share in the news from an old friend. After motioning for his women to prepare the meal, several others of the band scattered to do their part for the expected celebration that was sure to come. Now, seated in a half-circle near the lodge, they were joined by two other elders of the band, Big Man and Buffalo Horn. Big Man was one of the chiefs and Buffalo Horn was the keeper of the sacred bundle of arrows. Although he couldn't understand the conversation, Caleb was seated behind his Grandfather and watched the expressions and exchanges between the old leaders. Although he sat silent, he received many inquiring looks because of his raccoon-looking face with the black eyes. Looking toward the rest of the camp, he was surprised to see a white man, attired in buckskins, approaching the circle.

Charles Bent, one of two brothers that established Bent's Fort, a trading outpost on the Arkansas River in Colorado, was a long-time friend of the Southern Cheyenne and was returning from a trading expedition in the Northern fur territories and stopped at the village of his friend Big Man. As he neared the circle he was invited to join. He was acquainted with all the leaders and had previously met Black Kettle. Noticing Caleb, he greeted him in English and asked the reason for his presence. Caleb answered, "I am traveling with my Grandfather on a vision quest to the Medicine Wheel."

"Grandfather? Then you must be the son of Jeremiah, is that right?" he asked, but continued before Caleb could answer, "I met your father when he was traveling with old Scratch on their way to Kentucky. How is your father? Well, I hope."

"Yes, he and Scratch are both well. My father's family has grown now. I have a sister and a new brother."

"Well, when you see your father again, tell him Charlie Bent asked about him."

As the conversation of the elders subsided for a moment, another warrior approached the group and was welcomed by Yellow Wolf. Asked to join the group, Yellow Wolf turned to Black Kettle and said, "Do you remember my oldest son?"

Black Kettle looked at the younger warrior and turned again to Yellow Wolf and said, "This is your son? He appears to be a war leader with many coups, he cannot be the young man I last saw when we were together?"

"Yes, Black Kettle, this is the young man that bears your name. He is a respected war leader of our band and he has proven himself to be a wise and honored leader. He will one day take my place in the council." Turning to his son, he motioned to Black Kettle and said, "Black Kettle, this is the great warrior whose name your bear. Black Kettle of the Arapaho, this is Black Kettle of the *He´vhaitanio*." It was a rare thing for anyone to be given the name of another and especially of one from another nation and people, but the respect the Cheyenne had for

Black Kettle was well known and it was a great honor for his name to be given to another. It was also a grave responsibility for the one given the name as the honor carried by the name could not be besmirched in any way.

The celebration of old friends was an excuse for the entire village to participate in the feast and dancing that followed. Several times, young women made excuses to serve the visitors so as to give them an opportunity to flirt with the young grandson of such a respected visitor.

Caleb was not immune to the attention, but he continuously reminded himself of his required prayerful attitude and preparation for the vision quest. The reminder of his promise to Clancy to return to her was easily brought to mind as he unconsciously compared his vision of Clancy to the many flirtatious young women of the Cheyenne. The revelry continued well into the night, but Caleb turned in early and sought the comfort and escape of his robes in the borrowed lodge.

Rolling from his blankets at the first hint of light, Caleb stealthily made his way from the lodge and moved to the nearby cluster of juniper at the edge of the village. Expecting to be the only one there, he was surprised to hear the familiar chanting prayer of his Grandfather. He thought he left the old man in the lodge, but the bundle of blankets was apparently empty and his Grandfather had preceded him to greet the dawn. After tending to his necessary comforts, Caleb again found a seat on a large boulder and spent his required time greeting his God.

With the rising sun over their right shoulder, the quest was resumed by Grandfather and grandson as they approached the notch between the rising rim rock -

crowned plateaus. The day promised to be a good day for travel with a cloudless sky of brilliant blue arching over the travelers of three generations. The horses and mule willingly distanced themselves from the village and penetrated the wilderness of this rugged terrain of scattered pinions and intermittent rocky outcrops and dusty sandstone cluttered hillsides. The smile on the elder statesman's face revealed his fond recollections of the time with friends and the many stories of their war time exploits shared. Turning to his Grandfather, Caleb asked, "Grandfather, I couldn't understand the language of the Cheyenne, but you seemed to enjoy the many stories. Would you share some of those stories with me? I would like to hear about the times you counted coups and fought the battles. And what did you do to earn the title of war leader and chief?"

"Ahh . . . grandson, those are stories for another time. It is not good to talk about those things to others, that is boasting. But when you remember those times with others that shared those times, that is different. Maybe some time we can talk of it, or maybe your mother will tell you of those times."

The manner in which he spoke told Caleb this was the end of that subject. Now was the time to again focus on their quest and not to look to the past. It was a lesson in humility that Grandfather thought to share with his grandson. *I think I understand. The custom of the white man is to brag about his feats, but with The People the feats are to speak for themselves,* thought the young man.

THE BIGHORN MOUNTAIN RANGE stretched Northward into the far distance with its staggered granite peaks that selfishly held the winter snow like the crown of maturity and old age. The shoulders of the mountains resembled the foothills of the Absaroka and the Wind River Range with thick patches of black timber interspersed with bald meadows of high altitude grasses showing a dusty green. The Aspen were leafing out to add splashes of bright green overhanging the white trunks of the thick clusters that sheltered the elk and deer of the mountains.

Caleb and his grandfather continued their trek by staying in the lower valleys between the rolling hills, flat-top mesas and broad plateaus that tenaciously hoarded what little water was shed from the snow-capped mountains. The scattered juniper, cedar and pinion were too independent to form thick forests and were instead stubbornly self-reliant as they stood as lone sentinels on the otherwise bare hillsides. Many of the mesas had crowns of rim-rock and sandstone cliffs that set them off from the rolling hills below them. Yet many of the ravines bared their souls with chalk white cliffs carved by the occasional flash floods of melting snows.

Ancient trails led them on a winding and twisting path through the almost barren countryside. Cactus of many varieties from Cholla to prickly pear found footing in the sand and rocky soil and now threatened to splash color against the pale browns and dull greens with their new blooms of bright reds and yellows.

The terrain was somewhat monotonous to the young man that dutifully followed his trail-blazing Grandfather. Caleb was leading the pack mule and mindlessly searching the surrounding countryside for any new sight or animal. A sudden movement at the base of a cluster of sage caught his attention as three grouse ran to hide but gave away their presence with their cooing and chirping.

Caleb immediately mimicked the sounds and the grouse froze in place with confusion. An arrow whispered across his view and pierced the plump breast of a bigger bird that fluttered in a flurry of feathers before finally laying still. Looking up, he saw a smile spreading across the face of his grandfather as he said, "It is good to talk to them, but it is better to eat them." Caleb was surprised at the speed with which his grandfather had brought his bow to bear and the accuracy of the arrow. He knew his grandfather was well known for his prowess as a warrior and a hunter, but Caleb had never been a close witness to his skill. *That old man don't seem to be so old. That was some shootin'. This trip should have him worn out, but he seems to have gotten younger with every mile we've traveled... maybe it was all that talkin' 'bout the old times with his friends that has his blood runnin' faster,* thought the grandson as he considered his grandfather in a new light.

The day's travel passed quickly as the sun seemed to be cradled on the far horizon, just waiting for a chance to slip away. A trickle of stream giggled its way from a small cluster of aspen and buck brush as grandfather led the way to a campsite for the night. Caleb tended to the horses and the packs while his grandfather gathered wood and prepared the fire. The sage hen was skewered on a green willow branch suspended over the flames with the help of two forked branches stuck in the ground on either side of the fire.

After a winter's long diet of buffalo and elk, the bird was tantalizing to the young traveler. Dropping the packs near the lone log by the fire ring, Caleb leaned his Hawken on the log with the beaded sheath dangling its fringe behind. Grandfather had plucked the bird free of feathers, emptied its carcass and was now rubbing his secret seasonings into the skin. Caleb had placed the coffee pot on a stone at the edge of the fire and was waiting for the water to start boiling before putting in the coffee that he was grinding with a stone near the log.

From below the aspen grove came a "Hello the camp!" that startled Caleb. Grandfather was not moved but looked at his grandson and quietly said, "Did you not know they were near?"

"No, Grandfather, I guess I was too busy with the packs and stuff," replied the lad. "Shall I answer him?"

"Yes, but be careful, I do not think them friendly."

"Yo! Come ahead on, if you're friendly," responded Caleb to the visitors, then picked up his Hawken and lay it across his legs, checking to ensure a cap was in place, he casually cocked the hammer. Grandfather stepped back from the fire but stood vigilantly surveying the visitors as they approached.

Leading their mounts, two men attired in buckskins neared the small clearing with rifles cradled across their chests. Their predatory grins revealed brown teeth, full beards, dirty faces and searching eyes. "Howdy! We saw a bit a smoke and hoped we'd find sumbuddy with some coffee. Looks like we shore lucked out, Skimpy!" said the obvious leader to his sidekick.

The talkative one was a broad shouldered, unkempt pot-bellied man of average height that appeared to be the type that was used to bulling his way through life. His buckskins were black with grease and worn thin in places, and draped around his neck was the usual powder horn and possibles bag. His belt held a skinning knife and his rifle was a well-used, flintlock Kentucky style. The one called Skimpy sported similar accouterments with a grin that showed more gaps than teeth. He was well-named with a lean frame that stooped a little and every step required considerable effort.

"Ya mind if'n we share yore fire? We got us a couple a jackrabbits but we ain't had no coffee since I don't 'member when, it'd shore help these scrawny lop-ears go down better," asked the big man.

Caleb had turned on his seat to point the Hawken in the general direction of the visitors and with a look over his shoulder at his grandfather, he nodded. Grandfather maintained his stoic expression and had not moved since they were hailed by the two men.

"My name's Bull Graham, and this here's Skimpy Smith. We been clear up to the Judith and got jumped by them skunks the Blackfeet. Lost purt near ever'thin' we had, guess we was lucky to git out with our topknots though." He paused in his comments and looked over Caleb's shoulder to Grandfather and started to turn his rifle in that direction but stopped as Caleb lifted his Hawken. "Boy, that's a Injun behind you! Skeered me it did. What kinda Injun is he? He don't look like no Blackfoot and he's lookin' a bit peek-ed."

"He's my grandfather and he is Arapaho," stated Caleb without offering any additional information.

"Skimpy, why'nt you take our mounts an' tether'm over yonder," instructed Bull to his partner. Caleb was casual in his observance, but noticed Bull's wink at his companion.

When Skimpy returned, he offered a smile and a slight nod to his partner and seated himself on a large stone on the opposite side of the fire from Caleb. Apparently, Skimpy's assigned task was to evaluate the mounts and gear of the quest travelers and his head nod indicated their worth.

Bull tossed one of the rabbits to Skimpy and the two began skinning and gutting the big-footed rabbits for the skewer. Bull was the talkative one and now attempted to set the youngster and his grandfather at ease with his continual stream of gab.

"So, where'bouts ya headed? You know this hyar's

Crow country and them devils ain't none too friendly," he paused waiting for an answer.

"Yup," was the only reply offered by Caleb.

"Talkative little bugger, ain'tcha?"

"Sometimes," said the grandson.

Caleb noted the rifles of both men were within easy reach of the visitors and though both were flintlocks, he also noticed the hammers of both weapons were at half-cock which readied them for quick action. A flintlock's action has a side pan with powder held in place by a frizzen, a movable piece that when struck by the flint will cause a spark and open to reveal the powder to the spark igniting the firing process.

With a hammer at half-cock, the frizzen is down and the powder protected so that the user only needs to bring the hammer to full cock and, using the double set triggers, he is able to fire the weapon much quicker. This meant these men were anticipating using these rifles soon.

Caleb's rifle was a Hawken percussion that only required a small percussion cap on the nipple that when struck would ignite the powder and fire the ball. With his hammer at full cock and a cap on the nipple, his action would be quicker and more deadly. Although the rifle was still partially in the sheath, the trigger and lock were accessible and the rifle could still be fired, although it would leave a hole in the end of the sheath. But the sheath was noted by the visitors and gave them a false sense of security.

The visitors had suspended the scrawny carcasses of the rabbits over the fire with small Aspen branches and they now sat back on their stone perches. Grandfather had not moved and remained standing a couple of steps behind Caleb's seat on the log. Furtive glances from the two visitors told Caleb they were planning to make their move soon and he felt he must do something to give him and his Grandfather the advantage in any coming action.

Standing up and cradling his weapon in his arm, he said, "Well, fellas, if ya don't mind, I need to take care of business, you know, I need to water the flowers. I've had too much coffee and can't wait." Intentionally turning his back on the two men, he casually strode toward the edge of the black timber. As he turned, he saw the two men look at each other and nod their heads. Caleb was counting on them being ready to make their move on his return, and with a look over his shoulder he saw both men beginning to stand.

At the edge of the trees, he quickly disappeared into the pines, stopped and facing slightly away from the camp, he let loose with a loud and perfect imitation of an attacking cougar's cry. "Rrrrowwweeeiiirrrrrrrrr" he screamed, then turning and running to the camp he yelled "Git him! Git him! It's a cougar an' he's comin'!" All the while, Caleb was running sideways and looking behind him and yelling. As he entered the clearing he looked back at the woods and let loose a short cougar attacking cry, then turned back to the men and continued to run. Both men were taken aback and lifting their rifles, looked at the edge of the trees anticipating the charging cougar. Putting their weapons to their shoulders and looking to the trees, they did not see the quick movements of Caleb and his grandfather.

Stopping behind the two, Caleb let out a bloodcurdling cougar's cry that scared the two would-be mountain men so badly, Skimpy wet his britches and Bull spun around expecting to feel the claws of a mountain lion. But he saw Caleb with his Hawken pointed at the big man's belly.

"Did you do that boy? Make that cougar cry?" sneered the bull of a man.

With a slow nod, he watched as the big man stabled himself in his stance. Caleb knew the big man was thinking about his next move, what he could do to take the youngster.

"Now, what'cha pointin' that thar rifle at me fer?"

"How 'bout you putting your rifle down on the ground and make your partner do the same," instructed Caleb. The big man was looking at the youngster trying to determine if he could take him without getting some lead in his middle. Caleb knew by the big man's lack of movement, that he was deliberating his action.

"Well now boy, there's two of us and only one charge in that there Hawken. Now here's what's gonna happen, you're gonna put your rifle down, and me'n Skimpy there's gonna take all your stuff and your horses and if you behave, we might just leave you alive and mebbe even leave you that thar mule. Now what'cha think about that?"

"You forgot about my grandfather."

That comment caused the big man to drop his shoulders and scan the tree line for any sign of the old man. Skimpy was also searching the surrounding trees for any movement.

"Looks like your grandfather done skedaddled, boy. Now drop that Hawken."

A grunt from behind him caused the big man to turn slightly and see his partner with an arrow through his neck and blood spurting along the shaft. As Skimpy dropped his rifle and grabbed at the bloody shaft, he looked at Bull with wide eyes showing more white than not. Skimpy dropped slowly to his knees and gave the appearance of melting into a puddle of blood and urine.

As Bull turned back toward Caleb, he was raising his rifle when an explosion and a cloud of grey smoke announced his death. A .58 caliber ball had busted his sternum, launching the big man in a tripping stumble over the carcass of his partner and landing with a breath-exploding thump against the large stone.

Caleb had not moved and as the smoke from the black powder thinned out and rose to the tree tops, he saw his grandfather walking from the edge of the trees holding his bow down by his leg with another arrow nocked in the string. He walked casually to the two bodies, kicked them both to ensure they were dead, then looked at his grandson, nodding his head in approval.

"I will get their horses. We will pull the bodies down into the sage, their stink will bring the wolves and coyotes. We will free the horses, maybe the Crow will want them."

Taking a deep shoulder-raising breath, Caleb made his way to the log and began to reload his rifle. His Pa always taught him, "Never be caught with an empty weapon, son."

With the extra fare for their evening meal, both Grand-father and grandson ate their fill and now turned in for the night. Caleb was restless as he thought about the recent conflict with the two men. He had killed before, but never a white man, and the taking of any life was not an easy thing. He knew he had no choice in what he had done but emotions swirled around in his mind and made sleep slow in coming.

THE LONG MORNING SHADOWS FROM THE Bighorns held the travelers in the cool of the morning as they continued their journey. There was little variety to the terrain with rolling hills split by many gullies made by snow runoff and mountain springs. They followed an up and down route with the many twists and turns to the ancient path.

Whenever they crested a hillock, Caleb would pause and take in the view of the green Bighorn basin that held the Nowood creek feeding the Bighorn River. In the distance, a course of deeper green betrayed the presence of the Greybull river flowing from the backside of the Absaroka Mountains. This was a plentiful land with a lot of game and ample greenery for horse herds and villages. This was also the land of the Crow people and was often raided by the Blackfeet from the North. The Crow were known for their large herds of horses and the Blackfeet chose to raid the Southern tribes for their mounts. But looking at the lush green below them, the valley appeared uninhabited and peaceful.

"We will soon come to the Medicine Lodge creek. We will follow that creek to the place of great medicine," informed Grandfather as he gazed to the northwest. "I think we will be there by midday."

"The place of medicine? Is that the Medicine Wheel you told me about?"

"No, this place is before the Medicine Wheel. It is the place where the ancients dwelled and left their mark. It is a place of great medicine, you will see."

Midday found them following the creek upstream through narrow, green valleys with cottonwood and aspen lining the banks of the creek. Rounded boulders in the creek bottom did little to hinder the downhill plunge of the spring runoff as it cascaded in many white water-falls. The gurgles and splashes made a cacophony of distraction as the travelers saw a narrow canyon before them belch whitewater into the streambed.

The trail worked around the scattered boulders and finally opened to a one-sided gorge with sandstone cliffs hanging from the red clay hillside. Although it was early in the afternoon, Grandfather directed them to a small cluster of juniper to make camp. Looking questioningly at his grandfather, Caleb asked, "Why are we stopping so early, Grandfather?"

"This is a place of great medicine. It will do us well to visit the ancients and gain strength from their wisdom."

Caleb wasn't quite sure exactly what his grandfather was speaking about, but he held his silence in favor of watching to see if simple observation might reveal answers to his unasked questions. After making camp and hobbling the horses near the stream and a large patch of grass with many new shoots of bright green, Grandfather motioned to Caleb to join him, and turned to a narrow trail leading to the cliff side.

A foot path appeared to be well traveled but there was an absence of fresh sign from either horse or man. Although the dusty trail revealed ample sign of deer and bear with occasional tracks from coyote and smaller prey animals, the only wildlife they saw were a few rabbits, chipmunks, and birds.

After being surprised at camp the night before, Caleb watched the trail and surrounding area for any threats but saw none. Following his grandfather, the youngster was surprised when he stopped without warning. Bumping into the old man, Caleb looked to see why he'd stopped. They were standing before a sheer cliff of deep red with many carved markings of figures and emblems covering the flat surface. The young man had never seen anything like this and now stood with mouth agape as his eyes roamed the stories in stone.

"What is this, Grandfather?" he whispered.

"This is the place of medicine. The ancients here long ago made these by carving with stone upon stone. No one knows how old they are for they were here before my grandfather."

Caleb moved slowly along the wall of ancient art looking from bottom to top with his gaze lingering on different figures of interest. He reached out and carefully traced the images with his finger, and his grandfather watched as he marveled at the sight.

Caleb mumbled in whispers as he spoke to the figures and asked questions of the wind as to the meanings of certain images. Turning to his elder, he asked, "What do these mean? I can see what some of them are, but others are confusing. Like this one with the diamond and circle, or that one with the lines all the same length and the arc with the crooked lines. Do you know what they mean?"

Motioning his grandson to join him as he sat on the slight rise of a creek bank, he placed his hand on the youngster's knee and began, "No one knows what all the signs mean, but we can understand some... that one with the diamond and circle means Great Spirit, the one with all the lines means a good summer when the grass grows tall. You will see another like it with short lines when the grass was not tall in a poor summer. The arc with crooked lines is a cloud with snow falling or winter. The arc with straight lines is a cloud with rain. You should look at this as a place where the ancients came and made their marks so we would not forget them. There are things to be learned as we see the past of our fathers. As we rest here and let the Great Spirit touch our hearts, we can grow and be made strong with great medicine from the past."

With a simple motion, he directed Caleb to explore and examine while he moved to a place of sandy soil in the shade of a Juniper to spend his time in prayer. The young man rose and started exploring. Eyes filled with wonder, he walked slowly along the cliff face and took in the amazing petroglyphs. There was a scene of warriors with bows and arrows lying in wait of an approaching herd of big-horn sheep. The crude stick figures of the warriors and the similar figures of the sheep were easily deciphered by imaginative eyes.

Another scene depicted a village of teepees and figures of men, women and children busy with usual daily tasks, women cooking by the fire, men smoking pipes, and children running with hoops and sticks. The more complex scenes with different emblems and figures caused a wrinkled brow of the investigator, but he continued his self-guided tour of this place of wonder.

Taking a seat on a large boulder, Caleb pondered the pictures before him and began to imagine the ancient figures standing with stones in hand and carving the images. He pictured lean men with breech cloths and hides of deer or bear draped over their shoulders as they stood and beat against the dark red cliff face.

He allowed his mind's eye to place a woman and children sitting on the same stone, watching their mates and fathers make his mark on history. *I wonder what was going through his mind as he made these images. Was he trying to tell his story or just let others know he was here? Maybe he was leaving a message for others to know where the animals were, or where he was going, or ? Isn't that what I've been wondering too? If anyone would know I was here? Was this a place of worship and did they worship their Great Spirit or something else? Hmmmm ...* The rattle of a stone caught Caleb's attention and he turned to see his grandfather approaching. Looking at the sky, Caleb was surprised to see the rapid approach of dusk as he didn't think they had been here that long, but apparently his exploration and introspection had consumed more time than he realized. Grandfather motioned for Caleb to join him and turned to make his way back to their camp.

Caleb was surprised to see two sage hens lying by the packs at their camp. Looking at his grandfather with a question in his eyes, the old man said, "They walked up to me and offered themselves and I could not deny them. So I took them for our meal. You get the wood and I will fix the meat."

Without argument or question, Caleb went in search of firewood and skewers for the birds. Within moments, he returned with an armload of twisted cedar and pinion branches and started the fire. The dried wood emitted little smoke and quickly leapt to flames for the two men to prepare their meal. This time they enjoyed an uninterrupted meal and soon consumed the meaty birds.

Grandfather told Caleb they would be at the Medicine Wheel the following day and said he should spend some more time in prayer. Going to separate places among the scattered trees, both men enjoyed some quiet time with their God.

THE WIDE TRAIL BORE EVIDENCE OF YEARS OF use with deep ruts and an absence of any vegetation within the confines of the path. Sometimes called a travois trail because of the width and the ruts, it could easily bear the traffic of a caravan. The trail of the ancients made its way to the top of the plateau through a maze of white limestone hillsides.

As the travelers made the crest, the view of the Bighorn basin to their left was an impressive panorama of greens framed by the distant mountains of the Absaroka and the near peaks of the Bighorns. The flat-top plateau that lay before them, held the Medicine Wheel at its point. Grandfather simply nodded at the ancient cairns and led the youngster to the edge of the grassy knoll and near a finger of black timber that contrasted with the white of the nearby limestone.

"This will be our camp and here we will begin," he stated somberly as he began to dismount. Without question, Caleb followed the example of his elder, dismounted and began to prepare their camp. Tethering the horses near the edge of the trees, he removed the tack and packs and brought them near the fire circle prepared by his grandfather.

"We need many long limber branches to prepare our sweat lodge," stated the old man without further instruction, expecting the youngster to gather the necessary limbs. Caleb did not disappoint nor question and walked to the edge of the clearing that held both Aspen and Spruce. The scars on the Aspen trees told of other times those limbs were stripped for a similar purpose and forced Caleb to move further into the woods. Using his Bowie knife as both a hatchet and stripping blade, he procured a hefty armload of stripped branches that were four to five feet long and from the size of his wrist to his thumb.

Taking them to his grandfather, he was pleased to receive a nod from the Shaman as he accepted the offering. Beginning to prepare the sweat lodge required tethering small ends of the limbs together and arching them into an oval shape made from the larger limbs. When completed, the skeleton of the lodge was about eight feet long and four feet wide with the arch reaching about five feet. While Caleb was gathering the limbs, Grandfather had started a sizable fire and placed several stone around and near the flames to absorb the heat from the flames. With the framework constructed, Grandfather now placed the structure nearer the fire and spread three hides over the top, securing the hides with rawhide tethers.

Looking at his grandson, Grandfather now

instructed, "Bring the things I told you to prepare, but leave your pipe here."

Approaching the Medicine Wheel, Caleb surveyed the structure made from carefully placed limestone rocks. Staring in awe at the impressive layout before him, he was amazed at the figure that was shaped like a wheel. With 28 spokes radiating from a center cairn of about 10 feet in diameter, the spokes joined the external circle with six additional cairns around the perimeter. Caleb estimated the diameter of the wheel to be over 25 paces across. Grandfather directed the young man to the cairn or small circle of stone that was on the Western most edge.

"This place is sacred and we honor the ancients when we come here. This was here before my grandfather's grandfather, and my father brought me here as I have brought you. You will be here," motioning to the circular cairn at the West edge of the circle. "Place the blanket down in the center, and the four flags in the four directions."

As Caleb obeyed, the shaman continued, "You will face the sunrise and I will be at that point of the wheel," he directed the grandson's attention to the far side of the circle. "Place your choke cherry branch and your eagle feather before you."

Caleb bent to place the items at the location directed, then turned to follow his grandfather back to the fire.

Using green forked limbs, Grandfather began to place the hot stones just inside the lodge and as he worked he also instructed Caleb. "Fill your pipe with tobacco and enter the lodge when you are as you entered this life."

Caleb looked questioningly at the shaman, and with a simple motion from the man, he understood. Retrieving his pipe and putting tobacco in the bowl, he disrobed and stepped to the lodge. At a nod from the shaman, he entered. The lodge was very warm but it wasn't until Grandfather entered carrying a buffalo bladder of water that Caleb understood. When the shaman was seated, he used a green branch to pass a hot coal to the younger man to light his pipe.

With the only light coming from the small entry and the bright coal, he successfully lit the pipe and drew a couple of breaths of the sweet-smelling smoke. Grandfather splashed some water on the hot stones and reached for the entry flap to shut off all light and retain the steam from the stones.

The old man's voice came from the darkness, "Offer the smoke to the ancestors and into the four directions." Caleb lifted the pipe to the four directions, took another deep puff and extended the pipe to the shaman. Feeling the touch of the mouthpiece, Grandfather took the pipe and repeated the offering. Returning the pipe he continued, "You will now begin your prayer. Do not release the pipe, it is the symbol of your Creator. When we leave here, you will go to the place prepared. There you will stay. The first night and day, you will pray for your life. The second night and day, you will pray for direction. Do not leave until you are certain the Creator has released you.

If you need to relieve yourself, leave but return quickly." The shaman splashed water on the stones to retain the heat and promote the cleansing sweat. Well over an hour later, the stones no longer produced steam and the Shaman threw back the entry flap to signal to the young man to leave.

Without speaking, Caleb crawled to the opening and feeling the cool air on his sweaty body, he staggered erect. Noticing his weakness, he clung tightly to the pipe and as his eyes adjusted to the bright sunlight, he walked to the distant cairn and his place of prayer. Dropping to his knees on the blanket, he faced to the East and watched as his Grandfather, now clothed, took his place on the opposite cairn about eighty feet distant.

In his weakened state, Caleb wondered how he would be able to withstand the long prayer vigil, but knew this is why he had come and he would do as needed. The slight breeze quickly evaporated the moisture from his body and he felt the warmth of the sun on his back as it dropped toward the far horizon. He could tell by the waning light that darkness would soon come but he began to immerse himself in his prayer. From across the circle came a low chanting that wavered in cadence and tone as the shaman began his prayer for the young man that sought the face of his God.

Well God, here I am. I don't know where to begin, but I was thinkin' about what my mom said, and Jeremiah and Pa, about makin' sure of things with you. It was when Pa explained this was your plan of salvation. I never really understood that before. I thought that it was okay if I just believed in God, but Pa said it was more than that. When he told me we are all sinners, and he showed me that in the

Bible, in Romans, because we are sinners we are all headed for Hell, he kinda scared me. Really, what he said was the penalty of sin was death, but a different death than I thought, he said it was death and hell forever and that really made me think.

But he went on to tell me that You loved me and You sent your Son for me, and that the penalty for sin was paid by Him and I didn't have to pay it if I accepted Him and what He did for me. Now, that really made me happy and I wasn't scared no more, 'cause he said if I accepted that gift of salvation paid for by your Son, then I would have my name written in Heaven and when I die, I'd go to Heaven too. Is that right, God? I think it is because Pa showed me in the Bible, that book of Romans, that it is true, and that's what I'm countin' on God. So, now that we got that out of the way, and I'm sure about Heaven when I die, what about now? What about my life now?

I do not know what else to say but my Pa says you know what's in my heart. God, I don't know what my life is supposed to be or what I am supposed to do. Grandfather says I am to pray for my life and I guess that's what I am doing, I just want to know what I am to be. I've thought about stayin' with Pa and Ma and Clancy and just livin' in the mountains, but is that what my life is to be? I remember my father and he was a doctor and helped lots of people but that also made my mom and dad sick and it killed them.

I remember those people that were on the wagon train and that preacher fella, and he and his wife were gonna help the soljers and Injuns and that's a good thing. Then those traders at the trade posts, they helped people get to their homes and helped other folks with supplies and such. Is that what I'm supposed to be, somebody like that?

Darkness had dropped on the plateau like a cold black blanket that obliterated any sight. A blackness that could be felt was unlike any Caleb had experienced, with a silence that was suffocating. The drawing of his own breath broke the stillness and brought the young man a reassurance of his life and his being. Searching the wilderness of the plateau, he noted the glowing embers of their campfire in the distance. Suddenly a shadow crossed in front of the glimmer and Caleb turned to see if his grandfather was still across the wheel from him.

With his night vision slowly improving, the white of the limestone revealed an absence of any figure. Looking back to the fire he remembered his grandfather telling him it was now a sacred fire and must be kept alive until the end of the quest. Feeling the chill of the night, Caleb drew the blanket around his shoulders and looked heavenward as the stars began to unveil their glory.

Facing the east, Caleb noted the first light of morning making its way to shadow the granite peaks of the Bighorns. During the night, drowsiness sought to capture the young man but each time he would shrug it off and continue the contemplation of his life. With his mind traveling the trails of the past, it was as if he relived his entire life; the joys and heartbreaks, the adventures and fears, and the many people that stepped in and out of his personal drama.

He thought about those people and what he admired and respected about them as well as those that revealed weaknesses and vileness or lack of character. Thinking of his Grandfather and Broken Shield and Pine Leaf and his Pa and Ma and even Scratch, he thought of the common strengths they shared.

Then, he began to consider his life as if he were standing apart and looking at this person called Caleb or Talks to the Wind. *What am I, what do others see in me that is good or bad?* He continued the self-examination and evaluation and he began to smile and realized the answer was revealing itself to him. *It's not what trade or job or occupation I identify with, that's not me. My life is what I am! What kind of man I am! It is what Pa calls character and what's that other word, oh yeah, integrity! It is being a good man! That's what I am to be, a good man!*

He realized the term "good" was more than just a moral man or a hard-working man. To be like Pa or Shield or Grandfather, a truly good man, by any measure and by any standard, whether that of the People or that of his own family but especially that of God! He wanted to jump up and shout but knew that was not what this vision quest was and he remained still and began to thank his God.

With no water and no food, the spiritual fast seemed to make the time pass more slowly. The revelation of what his life was to be prompted the young man to continue his quest as he considered and contemplated the molding of his life and the direction he was to take. He continued in his prayer and sought the face of God as he questioned and proposed.

He prayed and meditated using memorized scriptures from his reading lessons. As he worshipped and squirmed in his small place in the center of the cairn of limestone, he occasionally moved a stone or twig that fought against his comfort. Feeling another lump under his blanket, he lifted a leg to reach the object of discomfort and felt a book. He reached for it and brought it before him realizing it was his Bible. *Clancy must have put it in the blanket when she folded it up!* He opened the Bible and began to read some of the dog-eared pages that had meant something to him in the past.

As the sun crawled its way across the sky Caleb was oblivious to everything that stirred across the plateau. He did not see the small herd of elk that grazed on the new grasses at the furthermost end of the flat. A bald eagle circling overhead, emitting its short scream failed to catch his attention. A skulking coyote drug his tail through the buffalo grass as he searched for a field mouse for lunch and his passing brought not a flicker of the boy's eye. The chipmunk that perched on his hind legs and held his front paws together as he looked at this figure on the cairn stayed immobile as the slight rise of the young man's chest was the only sign of life.

With the Bible in his lap, the pipe held firm in his left hand, and a glassy stare in his eyes, Caleb could've easily passed for a carved statue. With the coming of another dawn, the young man stirred as the brightness of the new sun bathed him in its warmth.

Taking a deep breath, the young man dropped his eyes again to the pages of the Bible before him and read, *"Trust in the Lord with all thine heart and lean not unto thine own understanding. In all thy ways acknowledge him, and he shall direct thy paths."* Proverbs 3:5-6 These were words read before but now they were exactly what he needed. *God was to direct thy paths."* That was exactly what this quest was about, direction.

What he thought he needed was a clear-cut command or some guidance as to what he was to do, but now he realized he was to trust God and as each day came God would give that direction. *That must be what Pa was tryin' to tell me, 'Just trust God' he'd say. I never thought it could be so simple.*

Lifting his head and looking around he could see his grandfather seated by the fire. Looking up at the position of the sun he also realized it was well past midday. He stretched his legs, stretched his arms and began to rise from his place on the cairn. Leaving the eagle feather and the choke cherry branch, he gathered his blanket and small flags and walked to his grandfather's side.

The fire, the sacred fire as Grandfather called it, was now just a few embers that peeked from a pile of ash. Grandfather was seated on a blanket with his legs crossed, hands resting on his knees and his head bowed. He did not look up at his grandson as the young man stood at his side. Caleb stood with the blanket wrapped around him and waited for his grandfather to acknowledge his presence. With no response from the Shaman, Caleb thought he must be praying and quietly moved toward the packs and retrieved his buckskins. Clothed, he walked back to the fire circle and whispered, "Grandfather, I have finished my quest. Is there anything more to do?"

Again there was no response from the old man. Caleb reached down to gently touch the shoulder of his beloved grandfather, but there was a stillness to his figure that alarmed Caleb. Crouching down to look at the face of his grandfather, he saw the closed eyes and somber expression that spoke of peace and satisfaction. But there was no warmth, no movement, and he realized his Grandfather had passed over to the other side.

He had taken the journey he often spoke of with longing and anticipation. His earthly journey complete, his last moments were spent by the sacred fire, tending it for his grandson and the vision quest. *This quest was as much for him as it was for me. Good-bye, Grandfather, may the Great Spirit welcome you.*

Caleb dutifully fulfilled his grandfather's wishes by preparing the body for the type of burial used by the ancients. Building a platform of poles deep in the woods, the wrapped body of his grandfather was placed with his weapons on the platform to expedite his journey in the crossing over. Some would sacrifice his favorite horse at the base of the cairn, but Grandfather told him he didn't want that and would prefer his horse to be set free to roam the wilds with his spirit. Caleb acceded to his grandfather's wishes.

"I TELL YA, I WANT THAT REDHEAD!" EXCLAIMED Colby to his brother. The trio was lounging around the remains of the night's fire with Cormick and Miguel still working at the bones of the skewered rabbits they'd shared for their night's meal. Lazarus, the slave, still labored with the mules and their feeding.

"You're just asking for trouble, my friend. Eef you try to take the senorita, that man with her will hunt you down and keeel you!" said Manuel.

"Yeah, and he's probably got family or friends that'll help him, and if they get you they'll get us. I ain't in no hurry to get myself killed just so you can have a redhead," grumbled his brother.

"But look at it thisaway... we're talkin' 'bout joinin' up with another wagon train, and there ain't no train gonna want three uglies like us. But if there's a married couple, you know, a man and wife, and his friends, they'll be glad to have us. Why, I might even tell 'em we're Mormons like them others and she'd just be my first wife, I could even be lookin' fer more wives like some o' them had," stated the older brother. "We've been here for a couple o' weeks and we got plenty of meat smoked and we can make it to that tradin' post of Bridger's and get the rest o' them supplies we need and we'll be ready to join up with the first wagon train that comes through. And onct we're with a big wagon train, ain't nobody gonna be able to git us."

"But, how are you going to find her, senor? You don't even know where they went!" asked Miguel.

"We can try! He said they was near a Injun camp and it was back up in them hills, an' where there's a bunch o' folks, there's gonna be cookfires and cookfires make smoke!"

Cormick looked at Miguel and both shook their heads in disbelief. Cormick said, "Well, I'm goin' to the bedroll, I gotta get some sleep." He was joined in his pursuit of sleep by both men as they made their way to the bedrolls around the campfire. Lazarus silently returned to his bedroll beneath the wagon.

Neither Miguel nor Cormick were surprised at the determination of the older brother as he mounted up to begin his search. "Well, come on. It's gonna take all of us to get this done. There might be some Injuns that need shootin' or sumpin'. Now, let's get ta' goin'," commanded the self-appointed leader of the group of raiders.

Moving single-file along a narrow trail, the three men traveled without conversation, yet attentive to the surrounding terrain. Breaking the silence, Cormick spoke to his brother, "What makes you think we can get her away from a whole village of Injuns anyway? You think you can just ride in and grab her and nobody's gonna maybe shoot us or wanna scalp us or sumpin,'?"

It was a valiant attempt to dissuade the single-minded lust driven mad man, but Cormick was certain the argument would be ignored. That's the way it had always been, whatever Colby wanted he went for and didn't care about anything else. It didn't make any difference if it was right or wrong, he was just like their dad who said, *"If ya' want something' then take it! If you ain't man enough to take it, then you don't need it!"* With no response from his brother, Cormick continued to follow on what he thought was a fool's errand.

———

"SHOULDN'T HE BE back by now?" asked Clancy of her Ma that was standing at the counter of the kitchen area.

With a muffled chuckle, Laughing Waters answered the girl, "Well, let us see now. Your grandfather said it would take about a week to get there, and the quest will take two or more days, and a week to come back. It might be any day now when they return."

"I thought so, it just seems like they been gone a lot longer than that."

"Do you miss him? You want him back sooner?" asked Waters with a broad smile splitting her face. She remembered the long wait she endured when Jeremiah went east with Scratch and the joy she had felt when he finally returned. Knowing Clancy was in a similar anxious state looking for Caleb, she was pleased that her daughter had resolved her questions regarding her future with Talks to the Wind. Though both Caleb and Clancy were her family, they were not actually related to one another and Waters believed the Creator had brought them together. She would be very pleased if they became one as she and Jeremiah had done many summers ago.

Jumping up from her seat at the table, Clancy blurted, "I'm gonna go see if I can see him comin'."

"You mean like you did the past two days?" responded Waters. With a surprised look on her face, Clancy turned to her Ma and said, "You knew?"

"Yes, my daughter. I know you have gone to look for him. Where do you go?"

"Down the trail just below the falls, there's an Aspen grove on the hillside and you can see clear down to the valley and see most of the trail up through Sinks Canyon. I just sit and wait and look. I will see him long before he sees me." Turning to the big lazy dog, she instructed him to stay with Little John, then turned to the door anticipating a reunion with her beloved.

The previous two days, Clancy had taken up her vigil early, but today it would be early afternoon before she arrived at her place in the Aspens. Tethering her mount in the shade with ample lead to reach graze, she took her position on the promontory boulder and began to scan the valley below. The time was usually spent with both observation and daydreams as she thought about what life would be like as a wife and maybe even a mother. Fond memories of her mother crowded her thoughts as she languidly basked in the afternoon sunlight. Pulling her knees to her chest and resting her chin on her knees, she allowed herself to indulge in a pool of imagination and anticipation.

The three men were seated in the shade of the tall ponderosa at the base of the hillside rising to the North. Taking a late lunch break they held the reins of their horses that were snatching mouthfuls of the grass by the streamside. They had followed an obvious trail that was discovered at the mouth of a narrow canyon and Colby was certain it would lead them to the redhead, but they had arrived at the end of the valley where the stream cascaded down a steep waterfall and the trail crisscrossed the hillside before them.

Miguel stood with a puzzled expression on his face and turned to look up the steep hillside. He thought he heard the clatter of hooves on rocks and he moved away from the ponderosa for a better view of the hillside with its scattered groves of Aspen. A movement caught his eye and leaning back to see a little better, he smiled and motioned the brothers to join him. Standing almost shoulder to shoulder, the three watched as a spotted horse traversed the trail toward the higher grove of Aspen. The redheaded rider was evident and the men knew their quarry was within reach. Careful not to reveal themselves, they continued to watch and survey the hillside for a possible route to the top. Each one leaned one way or another to peer around the intervening trees and search for a trail or a giveaway for their plan to take shape.

A nicker from the appaloosa in the Aspen caught Clancy's attention causing her to turn back to see what had stirred her horse. Standing still with head erect and ears forward, the mare's gaze was fixed on something uphill from the grove. Looking toward the hillside, Clancy saw nothing alarming, but she spun around on the boulder, dropped her legs to the side and walked back to still her horse.

As she reached to stroke the animal's face, she flinched and raised her head in alarm as a hand clasped over Clancy's mouth and an arm pinned her elbow to her side dragging her back from the horse. With a thrill of terror, she fought her captor by flailing her free arm and kicking back against his legs.

"Whoa, little lady, it ain't gonna do you no good to fight me. I got you, so quit all yore kickin' and swingin'," came the gravelly voice of Colby Jefferson. It was then she saw the younger brother coming from the trees to help his brother in the escapade. Seeing her appaloosa turn its head to look uphill again, she heard the clatter of rocks and twisted to see the Mexican riding his horse and leading the brother's two mounts as they worked their way down the hillside toward the Aspen grove.

"Now, if you stop yore fightin', I'll take my hand off'n yore mouth, can ya' do that?" proposed the burly brother. Clancy nodded her head as she realized fighting with three abductors would not accomplish anything.

"What're ya gonna do now, Colby?" asked Cormick of his brother.

"Well, first we're gonna tie her hands, then put her on

that there spotted pony and we'll be gittin' outta here, real quick like."

"What are you gonna do with me? You can't take me, my family will come after you and when they find you they'll kill you. You better let me go or they'll have the whole Arapaho nation after you!" threatened Clancy. The fear that filled her made her talk fast and loud and she searched their faces for any indication of their intentions. She would fight at every chance and would absolutely not submit willingly to anything they had in mind. *They don't know what they're in for from a redheaded, Irish woman!* she thought.

With her hands bound at the wrists, Colby lifted her to her saddle and reached for the reins to lead the horse back to the trail. With Miguel taking the lead and Colby trailing Clancy's mount, Cormick brought up the rear as the abductors started their flight from the narrow canyon of the Popo Agie creek. As they exited the canyon, dusk was settling over the valley but they easily found the trail that would lead them back to their camp and wagon. Looking at the cloud- filled sky, Miguel said, "We should hurry, with all these clouds there will not be any moonlight to show the way." The two brothers raised their eyes to the sky to see the grey clouds gathering over the West end of the long valley.

DARKNESS CLOAKED THE ENTRY TO THE canyon of the Popo Agie, but Caleb followed the familiar trail using intermittent moonlight and keeping the Mighty Hunter constellation over his left shoulder. Knowing he was hours away from the cabin hastened him as he anticipated the smile of Clancy at his homecoming.

With her image before him, Caleb was warmed as he thought of the promise their future together held. But the thought of his Ma and the news he must share about Grandfather weighed heavily on his heart. The mix of emotions was troubling; he was happy for his Grandfather that he was where he had wanted to be, but sad over the loss of his shaman and mentor, as well as his beloved grandfather. He was also burdened by the thought of the loss his Ma, Laughing Waters, would bear. High on the black skeleton of a snag of Ponderosa pine, a horned owl asked questions of the darkness and the traveler that disturbed his night-time hunt.

Quietly entering the clearing he made his way to the

corral to release his animals into the protective enclosure. Stripping the mule of the packs and his horse of its tack, then throwing the saddle bags over his shoulder and with a parfleche in one hand and his Hawken in the other, he walked to the cabin. Expecting to push the door open and surprise his family, he was startled when a voice came from the side of the cabin, "Been lookin' fer ya fer a while now, Squirt. Good ta have ya back home," growled Scratch as he joined him at the door. Pushing it open for the young man, he stepped back to allow him to enter the cabin with the welcoming fire blazing in the fireplace. His pa and ma stood up from the table, both with broad smiles to bid him welcome. Looking past her son and locking eyes with Scratch, Waters saw his negative nod as he dropped his eyes to the floor. Turning back to Caleb who was dropping his gear by the door, she spread wide her arms for her welcome home hug. Without disappointing his Ma, Caleb gladly gave her a big hug and stretched out a hand for a handshake from his Pa.

Both parents examined the expression on their son's face and easily determined there was something weighing upon the young man, but they were willing to give him time to share as they began the usual query. "Did you find the answers you sought?" asked Waters.

Pondering his response for a moment, Caleb replied, "The quest revealed much to me."

Noting his calculated answer, she inquired, "And did your Grandfather open your eyes and your mind like a shaman does on such a quest?"

"I learned much from my Grandfather, and I have much to tell you," said Caleb as he dropped his head and took a deep breath. He looked at Waters and began to tell her of the final journey taken by her father. As he finished his recitation of the days at the sacred place of the ancients, the room in the cabin was still and the quiet was interrupted by the laughter of a small child laying on his fur rug by the big black dog.

"It is as I thought it would be," spoke Waters quietly with her head bowed as she stared at her folded hands in her lap. Jeremiah rose and went to stand behind his wife, resting his hands on her shoulders to give some comfort.

Caleb began recounting the days prior to their arrival at the Medicine Wheel, the visit with the Cheyenne and meeting Black Kettle's namesake, the conflict with the mountain men, and how Black Thunder reveled in both the visit and the conflict and how he acted twenty years younger. Caleb smiled at the thought of his days together with his grandfather and said to his ma, "He helped me to understand many things and I will treasure those days for the rest of my life."

The expression on the face of his ma suddenly changed as a new thought surfaced and looking around at her son as she asked, "Where is Sun of the Morning? Where is our daughter?"

"What do you mean? I thought she was here and I've been looking for her, where is she?" asked Caleb with concern showing on his face as he leaned toward his Ma.

"She went to wait for you! You should have seen her on the trail. She's been going down there every day for the last three days!" she exclaimed.

"No, I didn't see her, course it was dark when I came through the canyon. Where was she supposed to be?"

"She said she went to an aspen grove just off the trail across from the falls. It was high up on the hillside and gave her a view clear out into the valley. She said she would be able to see you a long way off."

Turning to his Pa, Caleb said, "I've got to go look for her, she could be hurt somewhere!"

"Son, it would be best to wait until morning. With the cloud cover, there's little moonlight and you can't see anything."

"But Pa, what if she's hurt, maybe bucked off that crazy spotted horse of hers, or who knows what else. It ain't like her to be out by herself like this!"

"Your horse is beat, you've come a long, way. Just wait till mornin' and the three of us'll get an early start. It'll be better then."

"My horse is fine. That long legged appaloosa can go all day and then some and never get wore out. Cryin' out loud, that thing'll ride full out clear into next week. I'm goin', you an' Scratch can wait till mornin' if you want to but the woman I'm gonna marry is out there and needs me," stated the young man adamantly.

The 'gonna marry' statement prompted Waters and Jeremiah to look at one another and smile as they nodded their heads to each other. Scratch chuckled from the corner of the table and said, "Tole ya!"

"Ma, there's my saddlebags," said Caleb as he pointed to the pile by the door, "can you fix some vittles and pack 'em? I'm gonna saddle up and head out." Without waiting for an answer, he was out of the cabin, leaving the door ajar and the rest of the family staring at the blackness of the night.

Within moments, he whistled from outside the door and watched as the door opened revealing his Ma with the stuffed saddlebags and his parfleche and Jeremiah and Scratch gathering gear behind her. As he strapped the bags down, his father called, "You go 'head on, we'll be comin' along right after. Take Two Bits with you, he might help you find her."

The big dog lumbered out the door and looked up at Caleb as if awaiting instructions. As Caleb gigged his mount, Two Bits took off at a run following the trail out of the clearing. It was a narrow trail but well-worn and easy to follow even in the dark night. With minimal moon light and contributing star light, it was familiarity that guided the anxious searcher down the trail. The big dog padded on without delay and disappeared into the darkness. The black-bottomed clouds filling the night sky held the threat of rain and Caleb wanted to find Clancy before the storm added greater difficulty.

Breaking from the trees, the stillness of the night was marred by the continual din and crashing of the nearby waterfall as the Popo Agie dropped from the heights of the mountainside. Peeking out from between the clouds, the moon winked enough light to show an aspen grove just off the trail.

Quickly moving to the cluster of white barked trees, Caleb dropped from his mount and began to scan the area for any sign of Clancy. Nearing the edge of the trees on the uphill side, the tracks of several horses were evident. There wasn't enough light for Caleb to determine how many horses or see any sign of footprints on the grassy area within the grove, but just the sign of many horses was unsettling to the young man.

He also noted these tracks were of shod horses, and that meant they were probably white men. The only white men that he knew of were the three reprobates they'd met in the valley during their the buffalo hunt. Caleb remembered the leering expression of two of the men and their obvious envy of Caleb being with Clancy.

With a clatter of hoof on stone, Caleb looked back towards the trail and spotted Scratch and Jeremiah making their way towards him. "What'd ya find? Any sign of her?" asked Jeremiah as Scratch dismounted and started toward the grove.

"Yeah, there's fresh tracks of several horses up here and they're all shod," said Caleb as he watched Scratch examine the clearing. He was a proven tracker and few were better... the old man was said to be able to track a duck across water. Lifting his head, Scratch said, "Near as I can tell, there's two, mebbe three of 'em. They took the girl right here," pointing to the edge of the grassy knoll near a boulder, "Looks like she was up on this hyar rock and they grabbed her after she come down. Ain't no blood, near's I can tell. But she fought 'em a little."

Reaching down near his feet he picked up a thin strip of rawhide, "Looks like they tied her up with rawhide. I think this was planned. Weren't no accident, cuz they shore wouldn't stumble across her up here. They musta been lookin' fer her, or someone like her."

"That's what I was thinkin'. 'Member me tellin' you 'bout those three skunks we ran into down in the valley when we was huntin' them buffalo? The way a couple of 'em looked at Clancy, I think they mighta been wantin' to grab her then."

"They've got several hours on us, so we better get a move on. You remember where they said they were camped?" asked Jeremiah of his son.

"Yeah, they said they wuz up at the head of that valley, near that spring-fed creek that comes offa South Pass."

The trio of man hunters started out on a switchback trail that led to the bottom of the narrow valley. They would follow the trail out of the Sinks Canyon and into the valley below to try and pick up any trail as they reached the flats of the lower country. Travel on the trail eased when they reached the canyon bottom, yet before they cleared the cleft the sky darkened and the trail was briefly illuminated by the distant flash of lightning.

A deep throated rumble of thunder echoed off the canyon walls as the men spurred their horses to a faster pace. Now at a trot, they exited the canyon and a flash of lightning was just enough to show Scratch where the trail of the kidnappers turned down valley and it also briefly gave him a glimpse of the tail of the black dog moving quickly on the track with his nose close to the ground.

THE ROLL OF THUNDER AND CLAP OF lightning before them told of the storm coming from the South. The black-bellied clouds seemed to roll towards them like a foreboding monster of the skies. Wind whistled from the pines that crawled down the mountainside to meet the scattered sage and pinion of the flats.

The first sprinkles came at them horizontally and splattered against their faces like darts thrown from storm gremlins. Their horses ducked their heads and leaned into the wet wind. Colby tugged on the reins of the spotted horse carrying the redhead and angrily cursed the animal for resisting his pull. They were followed closely by his brother Cormick and the Mexican, Miguel, who were complaining about the whole escapade. Chasing the darkness, Colby had been certain they would reach their camp before the darkness and the storm caught them. With the storm already upon them, he kicked his horse to a canter in hopes of reaching the camp before full dark.

Clancy's hands were tied at the wrists with rawhide

and the rain pelted her unprotected face. Closing her eyes, she held onto the saddle horn. Her horse was closely following the big bay of the leader as the rain and the adobe clay soil presented uncertain footing. The slightly rolling hills of the valley bottom and the danger of the slick clay-like mud was unheeded by Colby.

He was anxious to get to the wagon and get out of the rain, and thoughts of a warm night with the redhead blurred not only his vision but his judgment. Rounding a narrow bend in the trail that held to the side of the hill, Colby's big bay stumbled on a rain loosened stone in the trail. As the horse started to fall the big man refused to release his grip on the spotted horse. The shifting weight pulled both animals from the trail and onto the slicker mud of the loose clay.

Kicking his animal forward, he jerked on the reins to return to the trail and with that movement, the unsure footing dropped the front leg of the spotted horse into the hole of a prairie dog, snapping it immediately. Clancy was thrown over the head of the appaloosa and with hands tied together was unable to break her fall. Landing face down in the mud, she rolled downhill. Thrashing around and trying to stop her fall, she smacked her head on a boulder. Darkness swept over her as she lay on her side with the increasing rain washing the mud from her face. Fortunately, the slope of the hill was littered with larger stones that stopped her descent before dropping over the sheer bank to the rushing creek below.

Colby fought his mount as it tried to gain sure footing. Within moments, it stood spread-legged and trembling with its head hanging almost between its knees.

Humped over in the saddle, Colby rested both hands on the saddle horn as the rain drooped his hat brim over his ears. He looked back at the spotted horse standing three legged in the slick adobe mud, jerked the reins on his mount and moved towards the appaloosa. The big mare stared defiantly at the cause of her injury and watched as he drew his rifle from the scabbard and pointed it at her head.

The hammer fell against the frizzen and nothing happened but a slight fizzle and a puff of grey smoke that quickly dissipated in the rain. Colby yelled at Miguel, "Hey Miguel, come shoot this ugly thing, she's got a broke leg!" Seeing Miguel reach for his rifle, Colby jerked at the reins again to find the redhead.

Groggy from the blow to her head, Clancy opened her eyes to the rain pelting her face. Unsure of where she was or why she was here, she tried to get up and slipped again on the slimy mud. Careening over the bank, Clancy screamed as she fell. Colby was nearing the jagged boulders as he saw her move, then slip over the edge.

Pulling to a halt, his horse dropped his hind legs under him and slid about six feet with Colby grabbing at the saddle horn and the cantle. Again, standing spread-legged, the mount refused to move. With the increasing din of the rising flood waters in the creek below, and with no sign of the redhead, he pulled easy on the reins to turn his mount back uphill. Nearing the trail, he saw the downed appaloosa and looked through the downpour at his two partners. Shouting to be heard above the roar of the storm, Colby instructed, "Come on, let's get to camp."

"Wait, what about the girl?" yelled Cormick at his brother.

"She's gone! She went over the bank into that flooded creek. Ain't no sign of her!"

Standing in his stirrups to try to see through the downpour, Cormick wiped the rain from his face and shook his head. Dropping into his saddle, he kicked his horse to catch up to the other two, shouting in vain, "Hey, wait up! I'm comin'."

Clutching at the slimy mud, Clancy tried to dig her toes into the bank as she slid toward the crashing brown waves below. With fists full of muck, she screamed for help but none came and she continued to slide. Suddenly, her feet touched an outcropping of gravel and stone, dropping to her knees she found herself on a slight shoulder about four feet above the thin brown mud racing down the creek bottom. A crash of lightning revealed her precarious perch to be nothing more than a protruding shelf extending out from the sheer bank about two feet wide. There was nothing to shield her from the wrath of the spring storm that continued its onslaught. Leaning against the sandstone wall, she tried to look above her to the edge of the creek bank. She was both hopeful the men would rescue her and fearful of their return. Looking back at the rushing muddy water, she knew if the rain continued, and the flood waters rose, she would be swept off her refuge.

Darkness obscured the camp of the three would-be kidnappers, but the retreating storm flashed a last charge of lightning to illuminate the slight draw and show that what had been a trickle of stream by their camp, now flowed like a raging river. The terrain around them was a natural bowl that caught the spring water and funneled it to the oft-dry creek bed in the bottom of the valley. The red clay of the hillsides, and the mud of the streams were identical in color and the rushing waters now carried the dust of dry country into the mixing bowl of red slurry.

Crossing the muddy stream from the hillside, the three walked their mounts to the small cluster of juniper that sheltered their wagons. As they entered the grove, they quickly dropped from their mounts, removed the tack and threw it beneath the wagons, then crawled into the already crowded refuge to curl up for the night and, hopefully, dry out.

Sitting on one hip with her legs bent under her, Clancy watched the slowly rising water and began to pray. *God, I need you, I need you to keep that water away from me. You know I can't swim and even if I could, I don't think it'd do any good, cuz that water's runnin' pretty fast. I think this here shelf is gonna hold me, but I don't need any more water. Oh, and could you get Caleb to hurry up a little bit, I'm sure he's gonna come after me, but I don't even know if he's back from his quest yet. Or maybe, at least, get Pa to come after me. Really God, I don't care who it is as long as somebody comes, okay? Oh, and could you hurry up a little, that water's startin' to scare me.*

THE DELUGE CAUGHT THE MAN HUNTERS JUST as they broke out of the canyon and started on the trail into the lower valley. The trail of the kidnappers turned into the smaller valley that led toward South Pass and the men followed blindly in the heavy rain. Jeremiah, leading the pack, stopped abruptly at the sight of the big black dog sitting in the middle of the trail. Crowding alongside their leader, Scratch and Caleb looked at the dog that refused to move.

"I think he's tryin' ta tell us sumpin'," growled Scratch through the screaming storm.

"We better find some shelter, come on," yelled Jeremiah to his followers. With heads tucked to their chests and the brims of their felt hats drooping around their ears, all three turned off the trail toward the thick cluster of Juniper. Two Bits followed.

Working together, the men quickly fashioned a sheltering branch lean-to with a rope stretched between two thick junipers. Tethering their mounts to a picket-line somewhat sheltered in the trees, the gear was pushed under the thick branches of another tree and blankets were taken to the lean-to. Two Bits took his place at the far back as the trio huddled under blankets to seek rest. Scratch grumbled, "Yeah, nothin' like tryin' ta' sleep with a wet-dog smell."

The morning light chased the storm to the high country and rustled the man hunters from their shelter. With renewed energy and a greater sense of urgency, Caleb wasted no time saddling his mount and securing his gear. Jeremiah and Scratch worked with experience rather than haste and were swinging aboard their mounts alongside Caleb as the trio started for the trail. The relentless rain had obliterated any evidence of others passing and any scent for Two Bits to follow, so the men hung close to the trail with observant eyes trained on the hillside for any sign of a camp or other giveaway as to the whereabouts of the perpetrators. No more than a half hour later, Caleb, now in the lead, saw the carcass of the spotted horse. Gigging his horse off the trail and to the appaloosa's body, he looked for any sign of Clancy. Standing in his stirrups and turning around for a panoramic view of the scene, he was disappointed to see nothing but the mud-caked hillside, sage, and tufts of grass lying flat in the muck.

From thirty yards downhill, he could hear the rushing water of the runoff from last night's rainstorm and he noted the many boulders with mud and grass and twigs pushed up against them from the runoff. But he saw no evidence of Clancy. Scratch had dismounted to examine the carcass and said, "She broke her leg, prob'ly in that prairie dog hole. Looks like they shot her cuz o'that." Looking to Caleb he said, "They probly just put her on back o' one a'their horses and kept on goin'. We can get the gear offa the carcass on our way back, ya think?" Scratch looked at Jeremiah. With a nod, the mountain man grabbed the saddle horn and swung aboard his mount without benefit of a stirrup.

"Come on, son, we need to make time before they try to disappear. This valley ends in that bowl up yonder and if they have wagons, like you said, they're gonna play hob gettin' up these muddy hillsides. So, long's they keep to their wagons, we should catch up to 'em 'bout mid-afternoon. If we get a move on, that is," urged Jeremiah.

With another look at the carcass of Clancy's spotted horse, Caleb kneed his mount to join the men making their way to the trail. The only evidence of anything was ample sign of the previous night's storm with mud-holes and trickling rivulets. The sun worked at drying the muddy hillsides and warming the travelers, but it wasn't fast enough for Caleb. The treacherous travel on the mud slickened trail and the many detours around mud-holes and other obstacles were aggravating to the anxious young man. His mind continued to betray him with thoughts of whatever treatment his Clancy might be enduring. He knew she was tough and would fight, but there were three of them and only one of her. Her Irish temperament would be to her benefit, but he was sickened at the thought of her even being in the presence of the three men he remembered.

As he mulled these things in his mind, he noticed

they were where he and Clancy had downed the buffalo and where he first met the three abductors, and his mind took another trip into the past. Here was where they had talked things out about their future together and where they began to talk about their future. Now, he was fearful there would be no future together, at all.

With the morning light, Waters was reminded of her responsibilities. She would need to travel to the village today and give the news of their beloved Black Kettle's final journey. A mix of emotions drove her as she prepared for the short journey by packing a saddle bag with rations and necessities. Saddling her strawberry roan, she soon took to the trail for the Arapaho village.

The solitary trek, with her only company a squirming toddler, allowed Waters to indulge in memories of her father who was also her shaman and the leader of her village. He had been a mentor as well as a father, a teacher and a guide as well as a respected leader.

The memories were many, from her childhood and learning to use a bow and arrow as well as how to craft the fine weapon, to learning to ride and care for animals, learning respect and responsibility. Every memory brought a smile to the warrior woman now entering the village.

Going directly to the lodge of the new leader of the village, Broken Shield and his woman, Pine Leaf, she was greeted as she neared the buffalo hide teepee.

"Welcome, my sister," greeted Pine Leaf as she

reached for Little John and watched Laughing Waters dismount. Signaling to a boy that stood nearby, she motioned for him to take Waters' horse and tether him nearby. Waters looked to Pine Leaf and with a somber expression said, "Greetings to you, Pine Leaf. Is my brother, Broken Shield, nearby?"

Hearing the greetings from within the lodge, Broken Shield tossed the entry flap back as he exited the dwelling. Seeing Waters, he spoke, "Greetings, and welcome to our lodge."

"We must sit, my brother, I have news," stated Waters as she moved beside the willow branch backrest used by Shield. Seating herself and pulling her feet to the side of her hip, she looked at Shield as he crossed his legs and waited.

"Our Father and Shaman has taken his last journey to the other side. He now walks with our ancestors," she spoke softly and bowed her head. "My son, Talks to the Wind, journeyed with him on a vision quest to the sacred Medicine Wheel. Our Father tended the sacred fire and when the quest ended, so did our father's journey. Talks to the Wind tended to the body as he was instructed and aided him in the last crossing."

It was customary at the death of a leader for the people to have a time of mourning and fasting during preparation of the body and the traditional rites of the crossing-over ceremony, but with that already at the sacred Medicine Wheel, Shield carefully considered what the people should do at this time. Reaching before him to the cook fire, he rubbed a finger against the black of a burnt log and made a stroke of black across his fore-head. Standing, he said, "I will call for the council of elders, you will join me and we will share this sadness. There will be mourning, but that is all." He stood, and with a curt nod, strode away to summon the other council members.

Watching him leave, Waters turned to Pine Leaf and asked, "And how is my sister? Are you beginning to make preparations for the new family member?"

A smile crossed Leaf's face as she unconsciously dropped a hand to her belly and answering Waters said, "No, it is too early yet. I sometimes forget that I am to be a mother. And how is Sun of the Morning? Is she still wondering about Talks to the Wind?"

Waters shared the happenings of the previous night and today. She also spoke of her concern about the failure of the men to return with the girl. "They will probably be waiting for me when I return and all will be well," she reasoned.

Shield returned with the council members following, and Waters watched as they entered the lodge. Leaving her young son in the care of Pine Leaf, she followed. The announcement was not unexpected and some even said they thought the shaman had planned on entering the beyond in this way. After the conclusion of the gathering, each member upon exiting the lodge, reached for the charcoal to mark their foreheads as they left.

The news quickly spread throughout the village and an occasional wail would be heard as someone expressed their sorrow at the loss of their leader and shaman. As she continued visiting with Leaf and Shield, Waters realized the responsibility of shaman was now resting upon her shoulders.

The village would look to her for guidance in spiritual matters and for physical healing. She was comfortable with the healing part, but a little intimidated with the spiritual part. She had reconciled her beliefs with those of her husband and knew in her heart there was very little difference in the two faiths, but her responsibility *to* the people would be guided solely in the *ways* of the people.

She had allowed her mind to drift as she thought about this and was brought back by a question from her brother. Looking at him and his expectant expression, she said, "What did you say?"

"I said, do you want Leaf and me to go with you to find your men?" asked Shield with a mischievous smile betraying his thoughts.

"No, I believe they will be back when I get to the cabin, unless something happened to Sun of the Morning," she said with her voice drifting off. She realized she really was concerned about her daughter and fearful of what might have happened.

"If they are not there, I will come for you in the morning and we can go then," Waters suggested. Receiving a nod of approval from Shield, she rose to fetch her mount and with Little John sitting before her, she started on the trail home. With a wave to her two watchful friends, she kneed her mount toward the cabin. It was well after midday when she loosed her mount in the corral and walked back to the cabin with Little John on her hip. Pushing the door open, she thought how empty the cabin was and how empty her life would be without her growing family, including every member that made her family complete. She felt a tremor of fear as she thought of Clancy and wondered just where the girl was and what was keeping her man and the rest of her family away.

IT WAS SELDOM THAT THE RISING SUN CAUGHT
Waters abed, and this morning was no exception. With a
handful of pemmican and a hot cup of fresh coffee,
Waters sat on the front step of the cabin and stared wist-
fully at the break in the pines that held the canyon trail.
With the tops of the pines showing a slight glow from the
sunrise, she silently spoke a prayer for the quick return of
her family.

Turning at the sound of hoofs on stone, she was
momentarily confused by the approach of horses coming
from the uphill portion of the trail, but the bright splash
of deep red and white on the chest of the horses told the
identity of her visitors. An upraised arm and open palm
were seen when the greeting came, "Ho, my sister. We
have come to join you in finding your men. We Arapaho
will go and find the lost white men that could not find
their way home."

Following close behind Shield was the smiling face of
his woman, Pine Leaf and she too raised a hand in greet-

ing. Her laughter filtered through the pines as the two drew their horses to the front step of the cabin. Smiling and standing, Waters said, "Come inside and have some coffee. I will prepare to join you in this search for the lost white men." She chuckled as she stepped back from the door to admit her brother and his wife. Taking a seat at the table, the two helpers smiled as they watched Little John waddle his way toward them to get some attention. Leaf didn't hesitate to pick up the giggling boy and she sat him on her lap as his mother made the necessary preparations. Leaving Little John in the care of Leaf, Waters went to the corral, caught the roan and soon had the animal geared up for the trek. As they mounted up, Waters thought how quickly her prayer had been answered, for she had specifically asked that Shield would join her if it was necessary for them to go after the missing men and her daughter. The morning sun finally revealed itself at the treetops while the three worked their way down the trail through pines and aspen.

Although the journey started with laughter and kidding, all knew that anytime someone goes missing, especially in the wild of the frontier, any number of things could be the cause and none of them were pleasant to consider. Now moving in silence, Shield led the party on the path that paralleled the Popo Agie creek as it sought the path of least resistance to make its escape from the high country.

Breaking into the clear from the black timber, he paused before revealing himself in the open. Surveying the steep hillside before him and turning to examine the timber around him, he signaled for the women to follow.

He was uncomfortable with the slight disadvantage presented, as the sounds of the mountains were a part of the survey but the only sound that could be heard was the nearby waterfall of the creek dropping off the shear face of the stone cliff that marked the end of the Sinks Canyon.

The trail across the face of the steep rock-strewn hillside was bordered on the uphill side by a broad cluster of aspen. Often called Quakies because of the flashing leaves that never seemed to be still, the trees looked to be constantly moving. Waters had told Shield of her daughter's observation point and the trio now reined their horses toward the grove of Aspen.

The storm had held to the valley and the natural contour of the land did not allow much rainfall this high up the mountains. Although there was evidence of the rain, the earlier tracks were still visible to the skillful tracker and leader of the Arapaho. He walked slowly, observing the ground before him, occasionally dropping to one knee for closer examination, then moving to the uphill edge of the clearing, Shield looked at the furrows of sliding horse hooves and further uphill to the origin of the tracks. Turning back to the women, he said, "Three white men came and took Sun of the Morning. They left on that trail," he spoke as he pointed, "and your men followed. The girl did not go willingly." No other conversation was necessary and he swung up on his mount and kneed it to the trail to begin their pursuit.

Little John enjoyed riding with his mother and now, as the three horses followed the switch-back trail to descend the steep mountainside, he often pointed and continually swiveled his head to take in every possible sight around him. Seated between his mother and the pommel of the saddle, his legs pointed to each side and he held to his mother's thumb as her hand secured him before her. Attired in a complete set of buckskins, he was bare-headed and the thick lock of black hair accented the piercing black eyes that told of his unending curiosity. As a typical mother, Waters carried on a one-sided conversation with her son as she told of the wonders of nature around them. Under other circumstances, the sight of mother and son on a ride would be a source of joy to any witness, but this was a search and rescue journey that was not to be lightly considered.

Late morning found them at the mouth of the canyon and prompted Shield to drop from his mount to examine the trail before them. Walking and leading his horse, he scanned the ground for any sign of the missing men, finally spotting a track where a horse had slid in the mud. He motioned for the others to follow. Although sign was scarce, Shield did not waver from the trail before him and the journey continued. It was after mid-day when the intermittent tracks showed where men had left the trail and turned toward the trees.

Shield followed. Without question or doubt, the women used their heels to goad the horses to follow their leader as he made his way toward a thick group of juniper. Nearing the trees, the evidence of a previous camp was seen with the pine boughs they had used for shelter and the turned up soil from the horses.

"They spent the night here. It is a good place for us to stop and let the animals rest."

The women slipped from their mounts, loosened the cinches and handed the leads to Shield as he led them to a nearby patch of thick green grass. Walking through the trees and carrying the boy, the women tended to their comforts and spoke little. Both had been busy with thoughts of what might be found and they both feared the worst. Stretching out a blanket and laying her son down, Waters tended to the needs of her son while he chewed on a piece of pemmican.

Leaf watched with thoughts of her own future with children and secretly hoped she would give her husband a son. Shield returned and said they would rest for a short while before resuming their journey. The women gladly reclined on the blankets with Little John between them as they sought a brief respite from their travel.

All too soon, they were on the trail again as they followed the winding path that wound through the rolling hills of the valley. To their left, the rising red, sandstone cliffs were beginning to absorb the early afternoon sun and the ground beneath them took on the red hue of the clay of the surrounding hills. The scattered pinion and juniper were sparse this low in the narrow valley, but the area was littered with sage and buffalo grass.

Random boulders appeared to have been placed by some giant hand while bands of varying colors painted the cliff sides. Looking skyward, Waters saw several circling turkey buzzards and motioned to Shield. He nodded his head and continued toward the flying messengers of doom.

Without thinking, Waters held her breath as they

rounded the small hillock that hindered their view of the trail ahead. Seeing nothing alarming, Shield kicked his horse to a trot as did the women. Nearing the object of attention, they startled two coyotes that had busied themselves with the trail-side banquet and now, with tails tucked, they slithered away with wary eyes on the intruders. Pulling his horse alongside the carcass, Shield stepped down to examine what lay before him. Waters joined him as they held their hands over their noses attempting to assuage the stench of rotting flesh.

Even with the damage done by carrion consuming predators, the spotted horse was easily identified as the Clancy's mount. Waiting beside a nearby boulder, a badger hissed his disapproval at their interruption of his feast. Two buzzards hopped on impatient claws anticipating their return to the carcass. Shield and Waters backed away from the stench and mounting their horses, rode a wide circle around the carcass looking for sign. When Shield spotted tracks near the trail, he recognized them as those made by Caleb's mount and motioned for his sister to come and see.

Turning her back to the cliff and the streambed beneath it, Waters clucked her mount to join her brother by the trail. As he motioned to the tracks, he spoke, "That is the track of Talks to the Wind, they go on up the trail. This goes to the end of the basin and then up to the trail known as South Pass."

"There is no sign of Clancy here, they must have taken her with them. She still lives," replied Waters.

COLD, WET AND LONELY, CLANCY LEANED back against the sandstone wall that formed the creek bank. The darkness came with howling wind and driving rain that pelted her mercilessly, driving her to huddle up against the sandstone. The stone held some warmth from the day's sun, but it was dissipating rapidly. Drawing her knees to her chest, wrapping her arms around her lower legs and putting her chin on her knees, she leaned against the rough wall of stone behind her.

Looking at the fast moving water below her, the dim light of night would not permit her to judge the distance nor the depth. Crashing waves and the occasional scrape of driftwood robbed her of any possibility of sleep. *If that water rises much further, I'm in big trouble. Please God, don't let it get any higher, I can't swim!* She thought as if she were telling God something, He didn't already know.

But the thought of someone to talk to gave her a measure of comfort. With the noise of the floodwater, the howl of the wind, the continued pelting of the rain and her continuing shivers, the girl soon grew tired and even more anxious as the night slowly passed.

The morning sun pierced the blackness of her slumber, bringing warmth to her chilled limbs. She was surprised at having drifted off to sleep in the early hours of the morning, but the waters still raged below her. With the increasing light of dawn she was reassured by the cloudless sky and the decreasing level of the floodwaters. Slowly stretching her legs and arms, she surveyed her precarious perch and surroundings. The opposite side of the streambed was held in check by the rising sandstone cliff that towered overhead with its dusty red and tan horizontal stripes of color.

Looking at the stream below, it became obvious it had carved its way through the sandstone as her sanctuary shelf was on a similar wall of stone. Lifting her eyes, she saw the veined sandstone end with a layer of gravel-like soil that was topped by a thick layer of clay adobe. It was that muddy slime that had caused her to slip and fall to her present perch.

Running her eyes upstream and down, she realized how fortunate she was that her descent happened where it did as this was the only shelf that would hold her and had she been as much as five feet in either direction, she would have plunged into the floodwaters and been lost.

Slowly standing erect with her hands searching for something to lend stability, they moved over the rough surface finding nothing. Stretching her arms high, she could not reach the edge of the sandstone. The flat surface of the sandstone wall had been smoothed by the many floodwaters that had carved its way to the lower reaches of the valley.

With her back to the stone, Clancy slid down to sit again on her shelf. The morning sun brought much needed warmth and her wet clothes were drying with the aid of the morning breeze that also chilled the girl. *What am I gonna do? I can't climb out, there's no handholds or places to put my feet to reach higher, and it's too tall.* Looking at the water, she noted the high water mark was over two feet above the current level of the stream. The water, though still very muddy, was not the thick brown soup of before. *Maybe the water'll drop and I can get out that way.*

Looking upstream, she realized the possibility of that would be a long time coming. Although not as deafening as before, the roar of the water through the sluice of sandstone still prevented her hearing anything but the splashing din. *I can't just sit here and wait for someone to come get me, who knows what's goin' on up there? They don't know I'm down here and the storm would have washed away any sign, so I guess it's gonna be up to me,* mused the redhead.

Squirming around to find a more comfortable position, her thigh rested on an obstruction that caught Clancy's attention. Lifting her leg thinking only to increase her comfort, she saw a palm-sized stone. It resembled some of the stones projecting from the gravel layer overhead, but was a bit larger, flat and rectangular-shaped with jagged corners. She started to throw the stone into the water, then stopped herself before launching the projectile. Looking again at the stone, then at the sandstone wall behind her, her eyes lit up with the realization she could use this rock to carve out some hand holds.

Standing again to examine the wall, she calculated where she should begin. Thinking she would need both toe holds and hand holds, she started her work with the first toe hold just below waist high. With one corner of her carving stone, she began a back and forth scratching against the softer stone of the wall. After a few moments of effort, she looked closely at her work and was excited, *this is gonna work! It's gonna take me a while, but I ain't got nothin' else to do!* She resumed her carving.

The day crawled by and the sun that was so welcome in the morning as it brought the much needed warmth was now an enemy. Blazing from above and reflected from the opposite cliffs, the heat penetrated the buckskin tunic and melted the resolve of the exiled beauty. Alternating hands with the carving stone, her fingers felt the wear as blisters grew and took on the appearance of fresh, raw meat.

As she started to tire she also felt pangs of hunger. The combination of sensations assaulted her resolve and she crumbled into a heap of desperation and defeat. Her head drooping and arms slack at her sides, she thought to rest and maybe regain some strength. Leaning her head back against the wall and closing her eyes, the steady din of the water below and the warmth of the sun soon lulled her to sleep.

She dreamt of her Mum and Da and the years of her youth, running and playing with other children amidst games of hide and seek. Then she was falling and falling, grabbing for air and a sudden jerk snatched sleep from her tired body. Waking with a start, her hands flat on the surface beneath her, her head snapped from side to side. She sought reassurance that she was not falling, but was safe, and still on her private hidden shelf of sandstone.

Taking several deep breaths, trying to still her rapidly beating heart, she held her hand to her chest and slowly relaxed. Without looking down, she felt for the carving stone, found it and brought it to her lap. Looking down at the stone, she also saw the redness of her hands and realized the task of carving her way out of this sandstone canyon was more of a challenge than she had first thought. But with no other option, she slowly stood and studied her work.

Three holes were complete, in a staggered vertical line with one another, the lower for her foot, the middle one just to the right for her second foot hold, and the upper for her hand. Now began the more difficult part. She would need to use these holds to support herself as she tried to reach higher for another handhold. Placing her left foot in the lower hold and reaching high for the other, she lifted herself against the wall and used the second foothold for stability.

Then she began to carve another hold higher still for her second grip. It was precarious, trying to keep her balance with one foot supporting her weight, her left hand gripping the upper handhold for stability and her right hand trying to carve out another hole in the wall. Unable to use her shoulders as before, the work was done with lower arm strength alone. Progress was slower than before and she quickly tired and had to step back down to rest. Seating herself on her perch, she again surveyed her limited panorama. The water level was still dropping and was now at least four feet lower than the high water mark, but as near as she could judge, the water was still beyond her ability to navigate.

Looking at the position of the sun, she realized dusk would soon come and her ability to work would end with the darkness. The thought of another night on this shelf was intimidating but there was little to be done and her stubborn Irish resolve would not permit her to give up.

Standing again, she resumed the work of carving her way out of the canyon. By the time darkness hindered her work, the higher handhold was complete and she calculated that with another day, she should have enough handholds to get pretty close to the top. But as she looked at the layer of gravel and clay, the dim light of the rising moon sought to discourage her with this additional challenge.

THE WHISTLING WIND ROLLED COLBY FROM his blankets as the grey light of dawn painted the eastern sky. In his usual surly mood, he kicked each of his companions to wakefulness and started barking orders. "Lazarus! Lazarus! You lazy nigra, get those mules hooked up, we're pullin' outta here so, get a move on! Cormick, you and Miguel get the horses saddled and ready to go and get this stuff," pointing to the bedrolls and scattered packs, "in the wagons. We're pullin' out, get a move on!" With grumbling complaints, the men started their assigned tasks.

"What's got into you, brother? What's you're all fired hurry, anyway. We need some coffee 'fore we can leave, and how bout sumpin' ta eat?" asked Cormick.

"We ain't got time fer that, mebbe after we get on the trail oer the pass we can stop."

"Oer the pass? You mean South Pass, in this mud? Are you nuts?" complained the younger brother.

"Shut up and get a move on, I'm gonna check out that

194 / B.N. RUNDELL

trail back there. We should be able to make it with them mules pullin'," stated the belligerent Colby as he walked to the picket line to saddle his mount. Calling over his shoulder as he reined his horse towards the trail, he said, "And you better be ready to pull out when I get back, we need to be long gone 'fore them injun lovers get here!"

With the thought of others pursuing them, Cormick and Miguel hastened their work. Miguel went to the horses while Cormick gathered the packs and threw them in back of the wagons. The two wagons, one belonging to the Jefferson brothers and the other claimed by Miguel, had belonged to their parents. Both families were afflicted by Cholera as they traveled with the Mormon wagon train, but only the older members were struck down.

Burying the four adults at their campsite, the young men had spent little time grieving and focused on planning their escape from this wilderness. The original plan of the two families was to travel with the wagon train and start a new life in Oregon territory, as both families had a farming background. The promises of free land had drawn them, like so many others, to pull up stakes and head for what they thought was the Promised Land. Now, the young men were plotting how they could escape pursuit of the family of the redhead the trio had kidnapped. Lazarus, the slave owned by the Jefferson's, was an unwilling part of the entire escapade. Always mistreated, he did not know about the law of the territory that forbid the keeping of slaves, but continued in his role as servant.

Completing their tasks, Miguel and Cormick looked

at each other with the same thought and as Cormick grabbed the coffee pot, Miguel stirred up the coals and added wood to the fire. Sitting the pot of water at the edge of the fire on a flat stone, Cormick ground coffee beans under a hand-held stone. Hearing the water start to move, he lifted the lid and dropped in the grounds. Both men went to their saddle bags and withdrew tin cups and returned to the fire. With the water boiling, they waited anxiously for the coffee to brew. Hearing the hoof-beats of the returning Colby, they looked at each other and rose to watch him ride to the circle. Looking down at the pot, he glanced at the two men, then at the wagons where Lazarus stood waiting. He dropped from his mount to join the two in a cup of java. He waved Lazarus over to join them and the black man came with coffee cup in hand. As each man held a full cup with hands wrapped around the warmth, Colby began, "Cormick, I want you to drive our wagon and Lazarus, you take the other wagon. You go first Lazarus. I'll lead the way and Miguel, I want you to hang back and watch our back trail. I figger the fella that was with the redhead is comin' after us and mebbe bringin' some of his injun friends. I thought he mighta been here by now, but we kinda lucked out with that storm. Mebbe it wiped out our trail and he don't know where we are, but I ain't takin' no chances!"

"But Colby, we ain't got his woman no more, he ain't got no cause to chase after us," whined Cormick.

Looking at his brother like he was a half-wit, Colby said, "He don't know that. For all he knows we got her stashed in the wagon yonder. When she went over that bank and into the floodwater, she plumb disappeared and he ain't never gonna find her. If he don't find us, mebbe he'll just figger she ran off or sumpin' but I ain't gonna hang around to find out. "

"Oh, yeah, I see whatcha mean," mumbled the younger brother.

"All right then, let's get ta goin'," ordered Colby, "that trail down yonder swings around and back up this hillside and comes out on top, and from the looks of it, it'll join up with the trail over South Pass. If we can make it up there, we should have purty easy goin' but this trail is kinda narrow in places and it's purty steep too. When we get to the grade, you're gonna have ta' lay the whip to them mules now, ya' hear?"

Both Cormick and Lazarus nodded their heads in agreement and started for the wagons. Swinging the empty coffee pot then tossing it into the back of the wagon, Cormick stepped on the axle hub, then up to the seat, and grabbed the lines before being seated. With a signal from his brother, he slapped the lines on the mules' rumps and leaned back against the backboard of the seat as the mules leaned into the traces and started the wagon moving. Lazarus pulled his wagon alongside Cormick and with a nod of his head, took the lead. The trail followed a wide arc as it changed directions to move diagonally across the face of the red dirt hillside to crawl to the top of the flat-topped plateau. Once on top, the trail followed the natural grade of the hilltop and under the shade of the towering mountains at the end of the Wind River Range connected with the larger and more prominent road of South Pass.

The adobe clay of the trail was solid and sure when

dry, but after the storm of the night before, it was nothing but slick and unstable. With each turn of the wheel and each step of the mules, the mud caked on anything that dared to step or crawl upon it. The footing of the mules became precarious with every step packing the thick clay to their hooves causing the mules to resist moving and afraid to take another step. Lazarus slapped the backs with the leads and talked to the animals with, "Come on mule, come on boy. Giddup Blue, Giddup Jesse, you can do it boys, come on." But the mules resisted and Blue turned his head back to look at Lazarus with big eyes that asked, "Why?" Colby turned in his saddle and saw the wagon stop, then yelled back at Lazarus, "Come on! Whip those stupid things, don't pamper 'em!"

Yielding to the command of his master, Lazarus begrudgingly grabbed the buggy whip from under the seat, cracked it over the heads of the animals and shouted, "Come on mule, pull!" Again they leaned into the traces and dug their hooves in to pull on the wagon, and slowly it moved. Each step required all the effort the animals could muster, but it moved. Gaining another twenty feet, the grade increased and the animals pulled valiantly with each step slipping and sliding.

As the wagon hit the grade, the increased resistance made pulling more difficult and the mules leaned, but the combination of slick adobe, steeper grade, and tired mules made first Jesse, then Blue loose footing and fall to their chests. Before Lazarus could set the brake, the wagon began to slide backward. Reaching for the brake, Lazarus was off balance for a moment, missed the handle and fell with his shoulder striking the edge of the wagon bed as the wagon continued to slide downhill and close to the edge of the trail. The mules fought to gain their feet and pulled against each other, tangling their hooves and harness straps.

Looking like some kind of circus act, animals, wagon and teamster moved unwillingly downhill. The right rear wheel dropped off the edge of the trail and the tilted wagon crashed to a halt as the axle dropped on a boulder and splintered into several pieces. Then the axle severed completely, and the wheel with just a stub of axle, began to roll down the steep embankment and crashed through the trees.

The braying mules, now with the wagon stopped, were able to kick and pull themselves upright. Lazarus clawed his way erect in the wagon box and set the brake. Climbing down, his feet hit the muddy clay at the same time Colby slid his mount to a stop on the trail.

"You good for nothin' nigra! Why'nt chu do what yore told? I said use the whip on them mules and now look what'chu done! That axle's broke and we can't fix it." In a huff, Colby jerked the head of his mount around with the reins and started back toward the second wagon. Lazarus could hear him yelling at his brother telling him to pull around the wagon of Lazarus and get a run at the grade with his mules and, "Don't spare the whip!"

Following the wagon up the trail, Colby stopped beside Lazarus and said, "Unhitch them mules, and start gettin' whatever's worth keepin' outta the wagon and pack it best's ya can. When Miguel catches up, you can have him help ya cuz it's mostly his stuff anyway. You can either ride one of 'em or lead 'em, I don't care. We'll wait up on top." Without further comment he clucked his mount to follow the wagon up the trail.

Miguel and Lazarus sorted through the many items of Miguel's family and Lazarus watched as the Mexican made the difficult decision of selecting the few items to pack on the mules. Chests, pans and dishes, clothing and other keepsakes were left behind. Selecting just the items that were personal to him, Miguel made quick work of the sorting and packing and sent Lazarus on his way. Miguel mounted his black gelding and turned back down the trail to take another long look at their back trail for any evidence they were being followed. Lazarus mounted Blue and led Jesse laden with the hastily secured packs of Miguel's keepsakes and clothing items.

After several repeated occurrences of slipping and sliding, Cormick successfully navigated the wagon to the crest of the hill. Stopping on the flat, he set the brake and climbed down on the sun dried ground, leaning against the wagon as Colby returned to his side. The older brother stepped down from his horse and stood facing Cormick. "Well ya made it! I knew if them mules got the whip laid to 'em they'd pull it like they's s'posed to and by jove they did. Good goin' little brother."

The long pull up the mountainside took most of the morning but covered less than three miles and Colby was getting anxious about putting more distance between them and any followers. But he knew the mules and the horses would need a good rest after the difficult climb in the thick clay, so he loosened the cinch on his mount and put some hobbles on to let the animal graze while they waited on the other two.

IN THE MOUNTAINS, THE WIND IS NOT ALWAYS welcome, yet on the day after the storm it was a companion of the warm morning sun and worked in harmony to dry out the slick mud to make travel easier. Caleb led the small procession of man-hunters further up the narrow valley. Remembering his conversation with the three renegades about their camp by a small spring-fed stream, he knew they were nearing the men's campsite. Turning to his pa, Caleb said, "I think we're getting pretty close Pa, what'cha think we oughta do?"

Nearing the end of the red basin, they were on a trail that paralleled the creek on the bottom. Now, shielded from view by a slight rise in the terrain, Jeremiah scanned the area to calculate the next move. Turning to Scratch he said, "How 'bout you working your way a little higher up the hillside there," motioning to the right of the trail, "and if I remember correctly, this trail winds around and up through those trees to the top, so watch yourself. Me and the boy here'll hang close to the pinions and scrub oak, but we'll wait a spell so's you can work your way up behind their camp."

Scratch reined his horse off the trail and followed a slight ravine uphill to the tree line. Watching their friend move away, father and son soaked in the warm sunshine that took the chill off their bones. Looking to Caleb, Jeremiah sought to reassure the anxious young man, "Son, I don't know what we're gonna find up there, but ya gotta keep your mind on what we're doin', cuz if ya don't, you'll end up getting us all kilt. You understand?"

"Sure Pa, I'm just a little worried about Clancy. I've been asking the Lord to watch over her, but you know, I just can't stand the thought of her bein' with those men." Jeremiah nodded his head in understanding and with a muttered, "Umhmmm," turned to watch the timber.

Catching a glimpse of Scratch passing through the thick pines on the hillside, Jeremiah motioned to his son to follow as he reined his horse toward the scrub oak brush they would use for cover. Stopping to tether their mounts, the men carried their Hawkens across their chests as they walked to the crest of a slight knoll for a view of the campsite. Jeremiah stooped over to lower his profile as he neared the edge of the hill and slowly moved nearer, ever vigilant to any movement. Caleb mimicked his pa's every action and the two men stretched above the buck brush to scan the camp. It was empty. Before approaching, they did a visual survey to ensure there was nothing amiss. Hearing a whistle from their partner approaching from the uphill side, the two men stood tall and walked to the campsite.

Scratch stood beside his horse at the uphill edge of

the small clearing with his back to the graves of the cholera victims as if to shield the graves from the view of Caleb. Seeing the stance of the man, Jeremiah looked askance and received a slight negative nod from the man in return. Caleb was examining the clearing for any sign of Clancy and upon spotting the tracks of the wagons, motioned his father to come look.

"Looks like they had two wagons and they pulled out sometime early this mornin'," said the young man to his pa as he motioned to the retreating wagons tracks. "I ain't seen no sign of Clancy, but they prob'ly got her in one o'them wagons," he surmised as he stared at the tracks leading back to the trail. While the men did their looking, Two Bits circled the clearing sniffing for any sign of his best friend. Finding none, he moved to Caleb's side.

"From the looks o'things, I think they took that trail that winds around back o'these trees and up to the top," Jeremiah said as he motioned and turned as if to look up the mountainside. Scratch had joined them and suggested, " Let's get a move on, fore them pilgrims get too far ahead. I think they might have a 'to do' gettin' them wagons up that trail, slick as it is an' all." He pulled on the reins of his mount to bring him alongside and the old timer swung up into the saddle without benefit of the stirrup. "Well, come on then," he ordered.

A short while later, the men warily approached the broken down wagon at the edge of the trail. Searching the hillside and the thick timber, all three men were thorough in their survey. Realizing they were alone, Jeremiah stepped down to have a look-see at the wagon. Peering in from the wagon box it was evident the contents had been quickly gone through to select a few items to keep and there was nothing to indicate Clancy had ever occupied the wagon. Stepping down from the wagon he looked at Caleb and shook his head as he spoke, "Ain't no sign of her, and ain't no sign she was ever in there. They probably have her in the other wagon and from the looks of those tracks," pointing as he spoke, "they didn't have it easy gettin' up this grade, so I'm thinkin' it slowed 'em down some. We might come on 'em sooner'n expected."

"Give me a little bit, an' I'll scout on ahead. You come on after me pretty soon, but take 'er easy as you do," instructed Scratch.

It took just shy of an hour for Scratch to top out at the edge of the plateau and he reined in by the trees before showing himself. He ground tied his mount, and slowly moved to the edge of the trees to survey the land before him. Scanning the tree line as it framed the plateau-top he knew that anyone hidden could only be under cover of the dark timber. If the renegades were set on an ambush, the likely place would be at the far end of the meadow where there was both timber and scrub brush to hide their intentions.

Carefully examining every break in the trees and every boulder or patch of brush, he looked and looked again. Something caught his eye, something back in the trees aways... there, it was the dirty white of a wagon bonnet.

Barely visible through a break in the timber, the kidnappers had either hidden it or abandoned it well off the trail. As the seasoned mountain man scrutinized the area in the vicinity of the wagon, he recognized several likely locations to hide and lay for an ambush. Backing away from his observation point, he picked up the reins for his horse, mounted and turned back to intercept the other two as they sought to join him.

Back down the hillside trail, the three met up and began to plan their strategy. As Scratch detailed the terrain and the probable location of the renegades, he also suggested, "I think if we can come at 'em from several directions, them pilgrims won't be able to put up much of a fight. Tell me 'bout them three, Caleb, what kinda fellas are they?"

Taking a moment to reflect the young man began, "There were three of 'em and two were brothers. The older brother, I think his name was Colby, was the bigger one of the bunch. He was 'bout the size of Pa, but his brother was more my size. I don't recollect his name, but he acted kinda squirrely, ya know, like he was nervous or sumpin. Now the other'n, he was a Mexican, lean and dark with ever thing he wore black too. He was shifty eyed, kept lookin' at Clancy, made her uncomfortable and she slid over next to me cuz of it. I don't remember seein' no side arms, but they all had rifles. The way they carried 'em was like they was itchin' to use 'em, too."

"We'll just have to play it as it comes," Jeremiah remarked, then continued, "Scratch, the way you described it, I'm pretty sure I been up there on a huntin' trip or two. So, here's how I figger we oughta do it. Caleb, you go back down the trail and work your way up the end of the basin, that hillside's got lots o' adobe so watch your goin' but I think you will do it all right. When you get to the top, you circle around and come up through the timber from the south. Scratch, you go back the way you came, stay in the trees and make your way at 'em from the north. I'll work my way up through the trees and come at 'em across the flats. It'll take me longer, cuz I'll be afoot, and I'll have to injun my way across the flat. But they'll be lookin' at me so that'll make it easy for you two. Wait for me to open the dance." Nodding their heads in understanding, the two started on their round- about routes to the confrontation with Two Bits hot on Caleb's trail. Jeremiah found a small clearing in the trees, tethered his horse within reach of graze, and started his climb.

THE MORNING SUN APPROACHED PERPENDICULAR, casting the bright warmth into the narrow gorge that was now Clancy's perch. The night had passed slowly and the cold lonely darkness robbed her of any real rest. Catching only occasional brief naps between shivering spells, she now basked in the warmth of the midday sun. Holding to her highest carved hand-hold in the sheer face of the sandstone wall, she examined the layer of gravel and dirt above her head. Clawing at it with her carving stone, she quickly realized her climb was at an impasse. With the layer of gravel and loose dirt stretching five-feet above her head, she could see nothing to grip for further climbing. *Maybe if I dug into the gravel, a hole just big enough for my arm, I could grip the wall of the small tunnel and reach a little higher . . .* she thought.

The ledge that had been her bed and partial shelter clung to the sandstone wall over a yard beneath her feet.

With her arms tiring, she looked below her and to the stream further down, and started to move back to the ledge for a short rest before resuming her climb. The flood waters had receded and the noise from the stream was no longer deafening and with her head turned, she caught a sound from above her. She froze in place and stopped her breathing to listen. *There, that sounded like a hoof striking a stone.* Turning her head to try to hone in on the sound or to hear anything from above, she listened. *Is that voices? What if it's those men coming back? Or what if it's the Ute Indians Caleb talked about? Maybe it's Caleb!* "HELP! HELP ME!" she yelled. Noticing a slight echo from the cliff across the stream, she turned to the cliff to try again, "HELP! HELP! HELP ME!" she screamed. The echo sassed her back with a mocking rattle.

Her toes started to slip from and she quickly dropped to the ledge below. Rising from her hands and knees she cupped her hands to her mouth and faced the top of the sandstone wall, "HELP! HELP ME!" When the echo ceased its travels, she listened. Looking up at the edge expectantly, she cupped her hands behind her ears to search the silence for any hope. Nothing.

Laughing Waters turned her mount away from the stinking carcass and dug her heals into ribs to move her horse beside Broken Shield. Pine Leaf had waited patiently beside her husband and continued to talk to and play with Little John as he leaned back against her chest. The two were continuously giggling at each other and Leaf greatly enjoyed the banter. Shield spoke to Waters as he motioned to the hillside beyond them, "We will follow the trail for a short distance, but we should move up into the timber. This trail is too far away from any cover." As he turned to lead the three away, Waters said, "Wait! Did you hear that?"

"Something from by the stream," whispered Shield. Waters turned her head to look in the direction of the streambed. Turning back to Leaf and Little John, she watched as Leaf silenced the child with a snug hug. Waters turned her mount in the direction of the streambed and moved him with a slight knee pressure to walk slowly in that direction. She reined him to a stop and listened again. Nothing. Moving forward again, she stopped to listen again. In the distance she could hear the gurgling of the stream as it cascaded its way through the narrow gorge, but there was something else. Suddenly came a confusing sound jumbled by a chattering of echoes bouncing off the opposite cliff wall, but she was certain it was human and she struggled to make it out.

Waters dug her heels into the ribs of her mount to move him forward at a trot and stopped him well away from the bluff's edge. Dropping to the ground, she slowly moved forward listening for any sound to indicate the source of the cry. *There, there it is again! That's Clancy!* Quickly she made her way to the edge and dropped to her hands and knees to carefully approach the uncertain footing of the bluff overhang. On her stomach, she inched to the edge to peer over the narrow gorge. Almost directly below her was the upturned face of her adopted daughter, Sun of the Morning – Clancy!

"Aiiieeee . . . are you all right?"

"MA!! Boy, am I glad to see you! I thought I would never get outta here!"

"Wait, I'm going to get Shield so we can get you out of there."

Wait? That's all I've been doing, and what else could I do? thought the girl as she smiled in relief and happiness. Waters soon returned with Shield holding a braided rawhide rope. He dropped to his belly and slithered closer to the edge to investigate the problem. As he looked at Clancy, he grinned and asked, "You ready to come up or do you want to do some more digging around?" motioning with his chin toward the carved handholds barely visible from above.

"I've done so much digging I'm beginning to feel like a badger, so I think it's time to get outta here, if you don't mind," she replied as she stood with her hands on her hips looking up at the welcome rescue party.

Shield instructed Waters to fetch her mount and bring him as near the edge as was safe, then he dropped the loop of the rawhide rope to Clancy, motioning for her to slip it under her arms. "As we pull, you use your handholds to help," he instructed.

Turning to Waters, he told her to dally the end of the rawhide around the saddle horn and lead her mount slowly away. As the rope became taut, Clancy leaned back against it and used her foot holds and hand holds to help. Within moments, she stood atop the bluff and quickly dropped the rope from her chest and threw her arms around her Ma and hugged her as tight as she could. "Thank you, thank you, thank you! I thought I would never get out of there." Looking around, she saw only Waters, Shield, Pine Leaf and Little John. "Where's Caleb, and Pa?"

"They were after those who took you. They thought as did I that you were with them," replied Waters. "We were coming after them and you when we stopped because of your horse," nodding her head in the direction of the carcass, "and we were just about to leave when we heard you yell."

"I thought I heard a hoof hit a rock or something, it's hard to hear down there with the water running over the rocks making so much noise. But then I thought I heard voices and I was afraid of who it was, but I didn't care so I started yelling. Thank God you heard me!" stated Clancy as she hugged her Ma again. "Uh, do you have something to eat and drink? I haven't had anything for days and I'm starving!"

"Yes, let us go over to that grove of trees for some shade and you can sit and eat and we can talk some more."

As they gathered in the shade, the animals were ground tied and cropped the grass contentedly, while Leaf returned Little John to his mother. Clancy busied herself with the pemmican from Water's pack and washed it down with fresh water from the water bag. Leaf and Shield were talking as they sat side by side in the shade of a bushy juniper. Shield smiled as she watched her famished daughter devour the handful of pemmican like a ravenous predator. The relief was painted on her face as her eyes and mouth wrinkled the corners of her mother's expression of love. With her initial hunger sated, Clancy looked up at her watchful Ma and said, "What? Ain't you ever seen a hungry person eat before?" stretching a smile across her own face. "I never thought this pemmican could taste so good."

Shield stood and approached Waters and Clancy with a somber expression as he began to explain, "You three and Little John should return to your cabin. I will go after the men. They might need some help and you three can get started back." It wasn't a question or an order, just a simple statement of what he determined to be the best course of action for all. Waters looked to Leaf and back to her brother, then to Clancy and Little John and nodded her head in agreement as she stood in anticipation of their return.

"My brother, I am grateful to you and your woman. Bring my man and my son back to me."

A simple nod to his sister sufficed, then he embraced his woman tightly, mounted his horse and reined him to the trail. Within moments, he disappeared over the small rise in the direction of the timber that skirted the hillside. Waters looked to Leaf as her friend led her mount closer and said to Waters, "I will have Sun of the Morning ride with me and you and Little John will share your mount." Waters secured her saddle bags and took a blanket from her bedroll, rolled it up and lay it behind the pommel of her saddle that had been Caleb's. Mounting up, she reached down as Leaf lifted Little John to his mother's arms. Waters placed him on the blanket in front of her and held him close with her left arm around his middle. Leaf swung aboard her mount and extended her hand for Clancy to swing up behind her. Soon the women were back on the trail in the direction of home.

The few hours of daylight left the women little choice but to make camp for the night before they entered the canyon of the Sinks of the Popo Agie creek. A thick cluster of Juniper and Pinion beckoned them off the trail and they soon busied themselves with making a comfortable camp. Clancy was tasked with gathering firewood and preparing the fire while Leaf picketed the animals and Waters fashioned a shelter with the lower branches of the larger Juniper and the scattered pine needles at its base. The women worked well together under the constant supervision of Little John and camp was soon made as comfortable as possible.

As Waters, Leaf and Little John gathered around the fire, Clancy already had coffee boiling and some cornpone in the skillet and a stew of jerky, water, wild turnips and onions simmering. Leaf looked at Waters and said, "This girl will make a good wife for your son. She will fatten him up so he'll be lazy and stay at home and get in her way. She will have to kick him out to make him bring her some buffalo," she kidded with a smile painting her face.

Waters nodded her head in agreement and laughed, "She has been a big help to me, almost like having another squaw in the lodge. If she leaves, I might have my husband marry another younger one to help me with the cooking."

"I could just see you letting another woman in the house with Pa. You'd scalp her before she got through the door!" remarked Clancy looking at her Ma over the camp-

fire. The women shared a laugh and enjoyed the camaraderie, but Waters was already thinking about the
emptiness of their cabin without the two lovebirds. But
that was the way of life, the young ones grow and leave to
make their own homes and have their own children, but
she would be rewarded with grandchildren and that
made her smile.

Seeing the glazed over eyes and the grin stretching
Waters face, Clancy asked, "And what's got you so deep
in thought? Are you thinking about Jeremiah again?"

"No, I was thinking about grandchildren."

"Grandchildren? We're not even married yet! And
you're already counting grandchildren?"

"That's the way of a woman, Sun of the Morning,"
commented Leaf, "even before our homes are empty of
children, we want to fill them again with grandchildren,"
as she rubbed her slowly, growing belly.

The women enjoyed the meal and continued their
banter throughout the evening with an undertone of joy
and expectation. Little John crashed on his mother's lap
and was soon deep in sleep with his occasional mutters or
movements betraying his travels through dreamland. As
drowsiness captured them all, the camp was soon still
with bundles of blankets making a circle around the
fading fire. Somewhere higher up the hillside, an owl
asked questions of the darkness and other mysterious
creatures added their harmonies to the night's chorus.

It was a restful night but it seemed all too short as the
morning soon winked over the eastern hillside and beckoned the slumbering camp to wakefulness. Slowly stir-
ring around to greet the day, each woman quietly set

about the tasks of gathering horses, gearing up and getting underway. Before mounting, they finished the warmed-up coffee and cornpone, packed the rest of the gear away and agreed it was time to start homeward.

The trail led them into the canyon and they stretched out single file as they began working their way up the switchbacks on the north side of the canyon. Traveling quietly, not out of necessity but more of melancholy, each woman was lost in her own thoughts but still watchful of their environment.

With the usual dangers to be concerned with, it would not be wise to be too preoccupied. Leaf and Clancy led the way but before the first switchback, both women dismounted and with Clancy walking ahead, Leaf led the horse. Waters wrapped the tail ends of the blanket around Little John and tied him to the pommel as she walked beside him with one hand on the boy and the other loosely holding the lead of the strawberry roan. The roan easily followed Leaf's horse as the group continued up the steep trail to the Aspen grove above.

Nearing the grove, Clancy stopped to look at the place where she was taken by the men. With her hands on her hips, she declared just loud enough for the other women to hear, "I hope they get all three of those scum. That kind doesn't deserve to walk the same ground as good people." The venom that came from the girl was witnessed by both women and caused them to wonder just what the girl had endured during her captivity. She hadn't spoken of the time, and the women had not inquired, but chose instead to let the girl speak of it in her own time and way. Looking back at the women that followed, Clancy dropped her head and stepped off again to continue on the trail home.

Clancy was quiet the rest of the way, but it was apparent to the others she was deep in thought. They assumed she was reliving the captivity, but Clancy was more involved in thoughts of her future with Caleb. She was visualizing her wedding and wondering what it would be like since she had never seen a joining ceremony among the Arapaho.

Since the people of the village were like her extended family, she assumed they would have that kind of ceremony and thought that would be what Caleb would want because that's the way it was with Ma and Pa. And as she thought about it, she didn't know of any other way they could be married.

And what kind of home would they have? Would they build a cabin like Jeremiah and Waters? She hoped so, not that the lodges of the people were not comfortable, it was just that a cabin was more what she thought of as a home. And what about those grandchildren that Waters was thinking about? How many children would they have? How many did he want? Clancy's expressions reflected her thoughts as they changed from smiles to stern looks of questions to consternation and confusion. Her thinking helped her pass the time and soon she realized they were entering the clearing and looking at the welcome sight of home.

Leaf decided to stay at the cabin with Waters and Clancy and helped Clancy with the horses as Waters took Little John into the cabin. They finished putting up the tack and carried the bedrolls, saddle bags and parfleches into the cabin. Each one busied themselves with putting things away and preparing the last meal of the day, but thoughts of their absent men soon surfaced as Clancy asked, "How long do ya think it'll be 'fore they get back?

THE SUN NEARED ITS ZENITH AS THE northeast wind blew over the trail on top of the plateau. The remaining surface moisture from the previous day's storm was evaporating quickly. Colby looked at his younger brother lounging against the wagon wheel and soaking up the warmth of the sunshine beaming down on him from a cloudless sky and asked, "Is that all you ever do is sleep? Every time I look at you, you're either sleepin' or lookin' fer your next bed. Come on and git up, here come's that lazy nigra Lazarus, an' we need to be pushin' on."

Cormick reached over his shoulder to grab a spoke of the wheel and pull himself up. Standing, he looked to the back trail to see two mules, one mounted, approaching. Leading Jesse and riding Blue, Lazarus neared the brothers and said, "That there Mex, he's agonna scout da' back trail to sees if anybody's follerin' us." As he drew alongside the brothers he started to dismount but was stopped by Colby's barking, "Don'tchu git down, we need ta' keep goin' and let the Mex catch up wid us. Cormick, git on up there," motioning to the wagon seat, "and foller me. We need ta try ta' git to the South Pass trail so we can git away 'fore anybody tries ta' catch us."

The older brother, the self-appointed leader of the group, was fearful of Clancy's beau and any kin of his and what might happen if they tried to find the girl. His plan of getting the redhead and making her his woman so they could join another Mormon wagon train had been spoiled when she was lost in the flood waters. Now his only thought was to escape pursuit.

Colby mounted up and motioned for the wagon and mules to follow as he reined his horse to the trail with the goal of South Pass. The going was easier with the trail drying in the sun and wind making the pulling of the wagon less tiresome for the mules. They lazily plodded along with the dozing Cormick rocking in the wagon seat. Lazarus followed behind continually adjusting his seat on the thin backbone of Blue in an attempt to find some degree of comfort or at least a less painful position. After less than half a mile, heads turned to look behind them as a hail from Miguel halted their progress. At a full gallop, he passed the wagon and slid to a stop beside Colby. With gasping breath, he reported, "They're comin'! There's at least three of theem. One ees that one that was weeth the senorita, and two others that look like mountain men! I theenk they want the senorita and we don' haf her."

"How far back are they?" asked Colby, looking around for some obvious cover.

"They were at our camp, wheen I took out, but I

could not go too fast cuz they would hear me. So we need to hurry and find cover so we can ambush theem," said the Mex with a sadistic gleam. The thought of shedding blood and watching someone die gave purpose to the bloody nature of the man who'd spent his youth fighting and killing.

It was that very nature that prompted his parents to leave their home and seek a new start somewhere unknown with the hope they could reform their son. Now the Mexican pulled his dagger from its scabbard and pretended to shave with it, then dropped it to his own throat and with a deft move pretended he was slashing someone's jugular. He grinned at the spellbound brothers showing his brown teeth behind the tightly drawn lips. They knew he would just as soon slit their throats as anyone's.

Standing in his stirrups, Colby surveyed the nearby tree line in search of an opening that would suffice to hide the wagon. Spotting what he wanted, he motioned to the trio to follow and dug his heels into his mount to canter toward a cut in the trees. The trail across the plateau was in the open and cut through the grasses and cactus while the tree line was about fifty yards west.

Colby angled the route to the cut and reined in by a stunted ponderosa, turned toward the wagon and motioned to his brother to pull the wagon further into the trees. As the wagon passed him, Colby shouted, "Pull it as far into the trees as you can, make sure it's under cover of some o'them big'uns."

He motioned for Lazarus to follow the wagon but stopped him as he drew alongside. "I want you ta' unhitch them mules and lead 'em all back into the trees yonder. After this is all over, you can start pitchin' camp." With a dismissive gesture to Lazarus, Colby turned to look on their back trail for any sign of pursuit. Speaking to Miguel he said, "Tether yore horse yonder, and come back here so we can pick our fight."

Feeling like a commanding general, Colby surveyed their location for likely shooting positions. With his head continually swiveling, he thought about approaches and defenses and when Cormick and Miguel came to his side, he began to share his plan. Under the shade of the ponderosa, he pointed past a squat spruce and motioning to the trail he said, "They might think we're on up the mountain and just keep on ridin' up the trail, so Miguel, you shelter yonder there behind that clump of boulder there. That way, if they's on the trail, you'll be the first to get a shot at 'em, an' iffn they hang to the trees, you'll be able to see in the tree line and mebbe pick 'em off."

Pointing to two logs just behind some scrub oak brush and a solitary fir tree, he instructed Cormick, "You hunker down 'tween them there logs and watch back in the trees, close along the edge thar and iffn they be sneakin' up thru them trees, you won't be seen and you can shoot 'em like ducks in a pond when they hit that little clearin' yonder."

"What aboutchu? Whar you gonna be?" whined Cormick to Colby.

"I'm figgerin' if they spot us, and chances are purty good they will cuz they been in these mountains a long time, they'll try to sneak around behind us and come at us from over yonder," pointing with his chin to the southern edge of the trees, "and I'll be in position to surprise them fellers. But if they don't, then I can scoot over here to whichever one of you's needin' some help."

Miguel and Cormick began to scan the area and think about Colby's tactics to see if they could improve them, but without any better ideas, they looked at each other, nodded their heads and moved to take up their positions. Colby walked back toward the wagon on the pretense of tethering his horse with Miguel's, but continued into the trees with his mount close behind.

He spotted Lazarus in a small clearing, tending the mules in his usual way by brushing them down and talking to them like they were his best friends. "That's a good boy, Blue, you done good, I don't care what Massa Colby says, you a good mule," turning to look at Jesse, he continued, "you is too, Jesse boy." Then looking at the other two mules he thought he'd better treat them with equal affection and said, "Course all yous is good mules, that means you Bella and you too, Fritz, you both is good mules." Colby shook his head and moved away into the timber.

Tethering his horse well back from the tree line, Colby cautiously moved to a slight promontory that would give him a good field of fire and observation of the back trail and the flats before them. Just inside the tree line and protected by a smattering of stunted trees and oak brush, his chosen position availed him good protection and vision. He seated himself on a sizable stone and leaned back against the trunk of the standing dead spruce. As he waited, he thought, *if they come from down yonder, I'll be the last one they see. I ain't in no hurry to die and iffn' theys three of them salty dogs, we might not make*

*it outta here. Mebbe if I took outta here now, I might just
make it away 'fore they come. Course, that'd mean leavin'
Cormick and the Mex, but neither one o'thems any good
no-how. Yeah, Cormick's my brother, but so what? I been
havin' to take up fer him all my life, an' now that Pa and
Ma's gone, who's to know?*

Continuing to think and consider, he patted the
pouch hanging inside his trousers that contained all the
coin from his parent's stash. Cormick didn't know his
brother had confiscated the small treasure for "safekeep-
ing" and future supply purchases. There was over $200
in gold coin and with only himself to be concerned about,
that would take him a long way.

With their remaining supplies and store of meat in
the wagon, if the other two survived, they could make out
and Colby's conscience was beginning to dull. His position on the promontory was visible to Miguel who was
stationed near the boulders adjacent to Cormick in the
trees. Sliding back from the brush, Colby looked back at
his horse and slowly moved through the few trees to the
side of his mount. Releasing the tether, he mounted up
and reined his horse further into the trees, took a
southerly bearing toward the South Pass trail and walked
his mount silently away.

Miguel sat soaking up the sun and the heat reflected
off the large boulders that made up his breastworks.
Watching the trail that emerged from the distant trees at
the crest of the plateau for any sign of movement, he soon
became drowsy. In an attempt to rouse himself, he looked
toward Cormick's position amidst the downed logs and
seeing his topknot swiveling in watchfulness, he looked

along the tree line to place Colby. The slight promontory that previously held the older brother now showed no sign of life and Miguel scanned the tree line for any evidence of Colby. There was none. No movement, no tethered horse, nothing to indicate the presence of their leader.

Mebbe he moved and I can't see heem, but where could he be? thought Miguel. Turning back to his look out, he thought he saw movement in the trees. Dropping his head lower he continued to scan the trees for any indication of the pursuing men but seeing nothing more, he turned back to again look for Colby. Looking at Cormick he spoke softly and said, "Can you see your brother? I theenk he moved or maybe left us, I can't see heem eeneewhere!"

Squirming in his log fortification, the younger brother sought to look southward to his brother's position. With brush and trees obscuring his view, he looked back at Miguel and shook his head, motioning to the trees as the obstruction. Looking around he stood up to get a better view but was still hindered in his efforts and dropped back down to his hiding place. Looking toward Miguel again, he shrugged his shoulders and held up his open palms to display his disdain.

Miguel shook his head in disgust, but knew they could not search for Colby until after the confrontation with their pursuers. Now it was just a time of waiting and watching. *Eef that snake has run out, I weeel catch heem and gut him from hees crotch to his chin!* Grinning at the thought of revenge on the older brother, his thoughts turned to his plans for Cormick as well. Miguel had witnessed Colby previously securing the pouch of money inside his trousers and had determined he would relieve Colby of that as well as take a certain pleasure in gutting the man.

He also knew that if he killed one, he would need to kill both of them and that just stretched his grin of antici-pation. But now, he must be ready for the others. Checking his flintlock rifle by lifting the frizzen and checking the powder in the flash pan, he lowered the frizzen and set the hammer with the set trigger. Gently placing it aside, he checked his two pistols in a similar manner. Satisfied, he lifted his eyes to again scan the meadow before him.

THE   LONG-LEGGED   APPALOOSA   EASILY
traversed the diagonal trail that led out of the red dirt
basin. Caleb reined his mount westward to follow the
ridgeline to the trees and his assigned avenue of attack.
Two Bits, in his usual anticipatory manner, led the way as
the horse cantered behind him. The two animals had
bonded the last few days on the trail and they behaved as
if they could read one another's minds.

Caleb let the big horse have his head as they moved
across the cactus and sage covered hillside rising to the
finger of pines that reached down toward them. It was
there they would enter the trees to make their way back
toward the apparent ambush set by the renegade kidnappers. Noting a shoulder that rose behind the trees that
would offer a good overview of the area, Caleb reined his
horse to take the higher route above the trees.

Within fifty yards of the edge of the trees, he crossed
the tracks of a horse moving rapidly to the south. Stopping his mount and dropping to examine the tracks,

Caleb looked at the hoof prints and easily saw they were of a single mount moving at a canter. Looking in the direction of the tracks, he could see nothing moving. Discounting the tracks for the time being, he remounted and continued up the hillside to view the tree line and meadow below him.

Scratch stopped his mount at the edge of trees facing an area of little cover that would have to be crossed to make his way into the deeper timber and on to his assigned point. Standing in his stirrups to scan the tree line further up the plateau, he dropped back into his saddle and gigged his mount to quickly cross the clearing and into the trees. Once hidden in the darker timber, he made his own trail on the slight tree-covered hillside toward the camp of the kidnappers.

Taking his bearings by the rising hillside beside him, he tethered his mount and began to work his way through the trees toward the waiting wagon. Detecting a sound and slight movement, he dropped to his knees to look below the branches of the surrounding ponderosa to find the source of the sound. Slightly below him in a small clearing stood four mules, eyes closed and big ears flicking back and forth, as they enjoyed the grooming of a solitary black man that busied himself in a one-sided conversation. One mule cocked his ears in Scratch's direction and turned his head to look in his way.

Slowly moving behind the nearby ponderosa trunk, Scratch remained silent and motionless for several minutes. Then, cautiously and slowly peering around the trunk, he began to move downhill and toward the wagon. He stopped with the wagon between him and the distant mules, waited and listened for any movement, finally approaching the rear of the wagon. With a stealthy move, he lifted the edge of the canvas bonnet and searched the interior of the bed and found nothing but chests and other gear.

There was no indication of Clancy. Slowly, he backed away and worked his way into the trees but only far enough to obscure himself from view of the younger brother Scratch had spotted lying between the logs. With a line of sight to the man below, Scratch settled in to wait for a signal from Jeremiah.

Standing near the crest of the plateau, Jeremiah rested in the shade of the nearby pines as he scoured the flats before him. The cut in the trees that held the wagon and probable site of the ambush was easily marked by the experienced woodsman but he continued his survey of the entire area. Caution was always the watchword of the mountains, for with any singular mistake or misjudgment, death or injury lingered near.

With his objective in view, he carefully mapped out his course through the scattered sage and cactus and strewn boulders. It was not an easy task he had chosen for himself, but he was confident he could approach within easy rifle range without detection. Crossing the open trail would be the most challenging part of his course. As he looked, he noted the slight rise and swales of the flat and determined he could lay low and make a quick traverse.

Cradling his rifle in the crook of his arms, he dropped to all fours and began his stalk.

Scattered sagebrush and cactus shielded him from view of the kidnappers until he dropped into the slight swale that meandered across the plateau. Still only on hands and knees, he laid his rifle across his back, secured it with a rawhide thong, and moved more quickly. The distance he must go was just shy of two hundred yards and it was no easy task on hands and knees, but within less than a quarter hour he reached the next point of his plan. Raising his head above the berm he looked toward the cut in the timber. He noticed the movement near the larger group of boulders offset from the trees and spotted one of the men.

While he watched, he noticed the two apparently talking and saw the second one rise from behind the logs. *Now where is the third one? Probably by the other edge of the trees.* He continued his comprehensive examination of the trees for any movement or give away, but there was nothing. Not wanting to move without locating the third man, he waited.

Caleb reined his appaloosa across the face of the hillside just high enough to look over the trees to the flats below. He spotted the white canvas bonnet of the wagon and the slight clearing in the cut of the trees. He also saw one man by the boulders and calculated the other two were back in the trees on either side of the cut. His knee pressure moved his mount down the hill into the trees and toward the cut, but before going too far into the timber, he stopped and dismounted to tether his horse.

Checking his Hawken, he set the hammer with the double set triggers and ensured the percussion cap was in place. Then, drawing the Paterson Colt from his belt, he checked the loads and returned it to its place. Remembering when his Pa had surprised him with the gift of the Paterson like his own, he smiled at the thought of the confrontation with the trader. Patting the Colt for reassurance, he started moving through the trees ever vigilant for the man they expected to be waiting in ambush on this side of the clearing.

With the years of experience hunting with his Indian friends and the many stalks of game, he moved silently through the woods, carefully placing his moccasined feet before him. As he approached the edge of the clearing, he could easily see the man among the boulders, then scanning the area, he spotted the one between the downed logs. *But where's the other one? Were those tracks I passed from him?* He stepped back to peer around another tree for a better view of the timber below him but there was no sign of the third man. He waited.

Jeremiah had slowly worked his way to a larger clump of sagebrush and a couple of nearby boulders that provided some protection. Peering through the aromatic foliage, he calculated his next move. The top of the Mexican's hat was visible as the man's movement betrayed both his location and his impatience. Waiting until it appeared the man was looking in his direction, Jeremiah stretched the barrel of his rifle and shook the far branch of the sage. He noted the man raise the barrel of his rifle to take a sight on the sage.

Again he moved the branch and within seconds the rifle spat smoke and a lead ball dug a furrow in the dirt beside the sage. Watching the action of the shooter, Jeremiah determined the man was quickly reloading and he thought he was armed with only one weapon. The rifle shot also told Scratch and Caleb the fight was underway. As Jeremiah anticipated, the man in the rocks moved his rifle for another shot, so Jeremiah shook the branch of the sage beyond the rocks to his left. Again the impatient man in the rocks fired and the smoke from his rifle temporarily obscured him from Jeremiah's view but also gave Jeremiah momentary cover.

He rose up and scampered to a small depression shielded by a clump of sage and dropped to his belly. Now, to the side of the pile of boulders used by the Mexican for cover, Jeremiah watched as the rifle barrel again protruded from the rocks. The impatient Mexican apparently thought he saw another target and squeezed off a shot resulting in another cloud of grey smoke from the black powder. Jeremiah quickly rose up and with his Hawken held before him, charged toward the man in the boulders. Startled by the movement, Miguel turned and drew his pistol aiming it at the charging mountain man. Both the Hawken and the pistol discharged with the pistol shot going wide because of the quick turn of Miguel.

Jeremiah's .54 caliber ball found its mark as red blossomed on the breast bone of the kidnapper lifting him off his feet and slamming him back into the pile of boulders. Dropping his Hawken to his left hand and bringing up his Paterson Colt, Jeremiah walked toward the crumpled form amidst the stones. Sightless eyes stared at the cloud-less sky and blood trickled from the corner of Miguel's lifeless mouth. Jeremiah exhaled with resignation and disappointment as he noted the youthfulness of the would-be bad man.

The initial shot from the man in the rocks signaled the fight was on and Scratch rose from his place beside the ponderosa and took a bead on the man in the log barrier. Holding his sight, he waited for the man to show any sign of battle readiness, but he continued to sit still in his bastion. Two more shots came from the boulder barricade and still Scratch held his bead on the man in the logs. After the two simultaneous shots and the cloud of smoke from the fight in the open, the log man rose and took aim. Knowing his aim would be on Jeremiah, Scratch squeezed off his shot and the roar and belching of smoke signaled the deadly projectile was on its way to the target.

The impact from the large caliber Hawken caught Cormick at the base of his neck and propelled him in a somersault over the nearest log as his weapon discharged into the ground. Certain of his hit, Scratch turned to see if the mule tender would join the fray, but no movement came from the trees in the vicinity of the mules and their keeper.

Caleb listened to the discharge of the rifles off to his left with the intervening trees providing a slight muffling of the explosions of the Hawkens. He could tell by the loud reports that only two of the shots were from the large caliber Hawkens carried by Jeremiah and Scratch. After the first shot, he carefully scanned the trees and the edge of the clearing for any movement that would give away the location of the third man, but the only movement came from the sudden alarming flight of birds seeking escape from the disturbance to their roosts. He continued his wait but, still no movement. Rising from his position, he quietly and carefully worked his way toward the clearing. He looked both at the clearing and continued his vigilance of the nearby trees. N nothing stirred as he broke into the clearing seeing his Pa walking toward him. Scratch came from his shelter in the trees and spoke quietly to Jeremiah as he continued to watch in the direction of the mule tender.

"There's a nigra back there with the mules but I don't think he's a part of all this. You come along and cover me and we'll see what he's up to," directed Scratch.

"Did you see any sign of Clancy?" asked Caleb of the mountain man.

"No, she ain't around an' it don't look like she's been in that wagon neither."

The three men cautiously approached the small clearing that harbored the mules and spoke loudly before breaking cover.

"Ho there, we're comin' atcha. Don't try nothin' foolish cuz we got you in our sights," directed Scratch as he led the way into the clearing.

"Nosuh, I ain't gonna do nothin' cuz it's just me, one only black man wit four fine mules. Ain't gonna do no shootin' cuz I ain't got nuttin' ta shoot wit," answered Lazarus.

As he approached the mule tender, Scratch asked, "Is there anybody else around? There were two down there and we know there was at least three of 'em, where'd the other'n go?"

"I dunno suh, I's been back here all the time wit my mules. This here's Blue and that'n is Jesse and the other'ns is Fritz and Bella. But down yonder they was three o'them. Miguel, Colby and Cormick."

"There were only two, the one was probably Miguel and the other'n was the younger of the two brothers. So where'd Colby go?" angrily asked Caleb as he stepped beside Scratch. "And where's the girl?"

"Girl? Theys ain't no girl. I heerd 'em talkin' but I don't know where the girl be," answered Lazarus, then continued, "an' I shore don't know where Colby went, but I thinks I heerd him take off 'fo da' shootin' started."

Turning to his Pa, Caleb said, "When I was snakin' round yonder, I cut a fresh trail that was probably his. Just one horse movin' purty quick off thataway," as he pointed in a southerly direction. "We ain't too far behind him and maybe he's got Clancy!" urged Caleb.

"I ain't never seen no gurl an' I'da knowed iffn a girl was 'round, yassuh, I would."

"Why are you travelin' with these kidnappers anyway?" asked Jeremiah of Lazarus.

"Kidnappers? Whatchu mean suh? I ain't seen no kidnappin', nosuh, I ain't. 'Sides I ain't got no choice cuz dey owns Lazarus," stated the black man with his head held low and refusing to look into the eyes of his questioner.

"Not no more they don't! You're in the territory and slavery is outlawed here. You're a free man Lazarus! Tell you what, you take that wagon back there and your two favorite mules and you just head out to wherever you want to go," encouraged Jeremiah with a broad smile.

With eyes wide and mouth agape, Lazarus looked from Jeremiah to Scratch and back at Jeremiah and said, "You ain't kiddin' Lazarus is you, suh? I shorely wants to be free, yessuh I do! But where do I go? I ain't got nobody nowheres."

"Well, right up there is the South Pass trail and that will take you to Oregon territory and you could hook up with a wagon train and pick out your spot and make you a new home. There's nothing to stop you because you are a free man," stated Jeremiah.

"Lawdy, that sounds fine. Yassuh, it do, an' I'se a gonna do as you say. Oregon here comes Lazarus!" With that exclamation, he led Blue and Jesse back toward the wagon and began to hitch them for traveling. Jeremiah looked the other two mules over and said to Scratch, "These two will make some pretty good pack animals, wouldn't you say?"

"Pa, what about that other'n? Are we gonna take off after him?" asked Caleb.

Before Jeremiah could answer, Scratch stepped beside Lazarus and asked, "Lazarus, there were some graves at that campsite back yonder in the trees, who's buried there?"

"Oh, them was the folks of dose boys, both of 'ems Mommas and Poppas. They was took with the Cholera several days back. Ain't nobody else buried there."

The sudden explosion and cloud of grey smoke accompanied the whistling lead ball that creased Caleb's hairline and spun him on his heels. Anger and fear fought for dominance in the mind of the young man as he realized he narrowly escaped death. Turning back around he spotted Colby at the far edge of the clearing and without hesitation Caleb lunged forward directly at the kidnapper now frantically trying to reload his rifle. Caleb was running all out with his rifle in both hands across his chest, and noticed the outlaw grabbing his ramrod to force the ball and patch down the barrel.

Without slowing his pace, Caleb watched as Colby withdrew the rod and started to raise the rifle to his shoulder. Anticipating the action of the assailant, Caleb continued and as Colby raised the rifle, Caleb fired his own weapon from his hip. Without slowing, he dropped the rifle and vaulted a downed log before him. Colby had taken the slug in his thigh and the impact caused him to drop his rifle and he now bent to retrieve it as Caleb barreled into him taking them both to the ground.

The kidnapper was taller and heavier than Caleb and tried to push him off, but Caleb drew his Bowie knife and brought the tip of the blade under Colby's chin, causing the bigger man to instantly stop his struggling.

"Where's Clancy? Where's my woman?" demanded Caleb with a snarl of anger.

"You mean that redhead? She's gone! The floodwaters took her down that gorge. You ain't never gonna see her again," responded the flatlander with a hideous laugh. Caleb pushed slightly on the blade bringing a trickle of blood from the man's throat. Colby squinted his eyes and began to laugh again and said, "Go ahead, do it! Do it!" Caleb was startled by the look of the man who acted like he really wanted the knife driven into his throat. "Do it, do it" he growled again.

Caleb started to push himself up from the man and with his arm now unhindered, Colby grabbed at the knife and pulled it quickly into his throat. The surprise in Colby's eyes mirrored that of Caleb's as he looked at the knife now buried to its hilt with blood gurgling and running from the neck of the choking man. Within seconds, the eyes glazed over and the body was still. Caleb rose to his feet, looking down at the figure that brought bile to his throat. Stepping aside from the body, he bent over and emptied his innards into the grass.

Jeremiah stepped beside his son and gently placed his hand on his back. Caleb straightened up and looked across the flats before them and said, "Pa, he said Clancy was taken in the floodwaters and she's gone."

"I was afraid of that son," and knowing there was nothing else to say, he simply stood by his son and waited for him to gather himself. He knew that his son had already suffered the loss of his grandfather and now this would be a heavy burden for one so young. But the making of a man sometimes requires trial by fire. Moving away from Caleb to give him some solitary time, Jeremiah walked to Scratch, explained what they now knew, and began preparations for the return home.

TWO BITS SENSED THE MOOD OF THE THREE men that followed him on the trail heading homeward. Caleb astride his big appaloosa was in the lead with Jeremiah close behind and leading the two horses of the kidnappers. Scratch brought up the rear with two mules, packed with the plunder from the renegades, in tow. There was no conversation and all three men were somber as their thoughts traveled the trails of the remembrance.

With the return of the questions that had haunted him before his vision quest, Caleb pondered his life and his future. Before this, everything seemed to be so clear. He and Clancy would be married and they would make their home here in the mountains and live near Jeremiah and Waters. It would have been a good life, but now there was nothing left for him. Maybe he would make a trip down to Fort William, the one they visited on the way back from Michigan territory, the one that William Sublette founded. Maybe there he could hook up with some trappers and give that a try, although his Pa never thought much of that life. At least he'd be on his own.

Or maybe he'd make a trip back to Michigan territory, but there was nothing back there for him. *God, I don't understand. I thought things were worked out. I spent that time on the mountain with you and I thought you clearly showed me what kind of man I was to be and that my future was with Clancy. Now you've taken her from me, why, God why? Now what am I supposed to do?* With the same thoughts tripping through his mind that he had already sorted through before his quest, Caleb shook his head and tried to concentrate on the trail before him.

Two Bits jogged along the trail with his head sweeping back and forth checking the scent on anything that might rouse his interest. The horses and mules seemed to pick up on the mood of the men and plodded along dragging their feet in the dust with heads hanging low. The sun was cradled in the gentle dip of the horizon and winking its farewell for the day. The shadows of dusk seemed to garner the attention of Jeremiah as he lifted his head to survey their surroundings for a possible campsite. Turning his head as if he was searching for something, he looked back at the drowsy Scratch and softly asked, "Do you smell wood smoke? I just caught a whiff of something and it might be a camp, maybe some of them raidin' Utes. Whatcha think?"

The query brought Scratch out of his reverie to move his mount alongside Jeremiah. Their talk caught the attention of Caleb and brought him to a halt to await the older men's decision. Scratch responded, "Yeah, I think I smell it too, can't be too big and with the wind comin' from behind us, no tellin' where it is."

Caleb reined his horse around to join the group discussion and said, "Well, there sure enough ain't no camp down in the bottom yonder, it's too open. And it ain't comin' from behind us cause of the wind and 'sides we just come from up there, so that just leaves somewhere back in the trees toward the hillside. As I recollect this area from when me and Clancy," a choke caught in his throat but he continued, "when we was down here after buffalo, not too far around that bend in the trail, we had us a camp back in the trees that was purty cozy an' outta the wind. Mebbe somebody else is at that same spot."

"Sounds reasonable, but who is it? And how many? Could be Utes from down South o' here on a raidin' party, or even Cheyenne from out on the flats and fer that matter, it might be some o' our own lookin' fer buffalo," surmised Scratch.

Jeremiah scanned the terrain before them. They were behind a low rising knoll that obscured their view of the area spoken of by Caleb and not too far away from the tree line. The trail made a wide bend to their right and back to the left to circumvent the rise of the knoll and keep the riders in the low swale of the valley. What provided them cover and obscurity also prevented their viewing the scene beyond the rise.

"Let's move back up in those trees and maybe one of us will have to injun up on that camp to see what we're gettin' into," suggested Jeremiah. Without discussion, the three men, four horses, two mules and one dog turned to

the trees for some cover. As they moved into the length-
ening shadows of the trees, the three men dismounted
and came together to talk about the impending action.
Scratch spoke first, "Why'nt chu two fellers stay here with
all these hyar animals, and I'll just injun on up there and
check out who our neighbors might be, cuz it shore ain't
gonna take all three of us for this one piddly job."

"I guess that's fair enough, don't you think Caleb?"
asked Jeremiah.

"Suits me, course iffn ya want, we could just make
camp here."

"Huh uhhh, not with that camp so close an' not
knowin' what might be thar. You'ns just sit tight fer a
spell an' I'll be back shortly," directed Scratch as he
turned and trotted into the timber headed for the bench
that would take him over the rise. Before they could stop
him, Two Bits loped off into the shadows after the mountain man.

When he neared the area in question, Scratch
stopped and dropped to one knee for a thorough survey
of the area. As he lifted his head to sniff the air, the big
black dog padded silently to his side and duplicated his
efforts. Turning his head to look at the beast, Scratch
whispered, "What are you doin' here? You better not get
me found out boy or I'll have to skin you." But the
scraggly buckskin clad mountain man knew the dog was
well attuned to the woods and was stealthier than even
the best woodsman. Catching a whiff of smoke, Scratch
and Two Bits began a stalk toward the source of the
campfire.

Several yards farther he sighted a slight glow of firelight against some trees. Moving even more cautiously, he stepped from tree to tree to gain a better view of the camp and to see what they might be up against. Nearing the site, he could only make out a solitary figure but he thought, *Sure 'nuff, that's an injun and where there's one, there's bound to be more. Now where would they be hidin'?* As he surveyed the area, the big dog took off bounding toward the camp and its occupant. Without slowing he charged at the figure who quickly stood up and turned to face the threat. Two Bits jumped up and placed his paws on the man's chest and began to lick his face as the man rubbed behind his ears and greeted his friend. The Indian spoke to the darkness of the woods and said, "Scratch, come to my fire before some animal of the night tries to eat your tough hide."

Recognizing Broken Shield, Scratch rose from his crouch and walked into the light of the fire to greet his friend. "Broken Shield! You have to be the sneakiest injun I've ever knowed. What are you doin' out here all by yore lonesome?"

"My sister sent me to find her men. She thought you white men were lost and needed help to find your way home."

Scratch noticed the meat broiling over the fire and said, "You must be mighty hungry, that's a lot of meat for one man."

"I knew you were coming and the antelope is waiting for you."

"Wal, I better go get them others 'fore they starve, specially that younger one. He eats like a grizzly bear!"

With Two Bits staying with Broken Shield, Scratch

trotted through the trees to share his find with his partners. The welcome news brought smiles to the faces of
father and son and the entourage made short work of
joining the camp of Broken Shield. They strung a picket
line for the animals, dropped their gear near the fire,
stretched out bedrolls and took a seat on the log and
stones near the fire circle. Looking hungrily at the
broiling antelope steaks suspended over the edge of the
fire, their mouths watering and their eyes searching, the
men were ready for a tasty meal. Little conversation was
exchanged during the business of making camp and now
with everyone chomping on the tender juicy steaks,
juices running down their chins, Shield inquired, "Was
your mission successful?"

Jeremiah glanced over at Caleb then answered his
friend, "Well, yes and no. We caught the men and buried
'em up yonder. There was another'n, a slave, that we let
have the wagon and a couple of mules and sent him on
his way. But, we didn't find Clancy. One of 'em said she
was lost in the floodwaters."

Shield looked at the three men and let his gaze linger
on Caleb, then spoke to the group, "No, she was not lost.
She is at home with Waters and Leaf."

All three men jerked their heads to look at Shield as
he sat with a stoic expression staring into the fire. Then
lifting his head, he could keep the somber expression no
longer and broke into a broad grin towards Caleb.

"You mean it? She's alive? She's okay? Really? Ohh. . .
thank you, God!! Wow! Did you hear that Pa? Clancy's
alive!" he shouted as he jumped up and bounced around
the small camp. "But how? Where? What happened?"

"Son, slow down, he'll tell it. Now sit down and be quiet so we can enjoy our meal and let him tell it," instructed Jeremiah and turned with a smile to Shield and gave a nod so his friend would share the details.

"You remember passing the carcass of her horse?" he asked Caleb and receiving an affirmative nod continued, "When we saw the horse . . . " and the story unfolded for the returning men as they absorbed the details of the rescue of the woman that had prompted their search. As he concluded he finished with, ". . . she wanted me to find you lost white men and bring you home safely. She didn't want to have to come searching for you."

Two Bits detected the change in mood and now paced the camp with wagging tail and slobbering mouth that caught the thrown scraps of meat. Flopping back down beside Caleb, he reveled in the absentminded scratching that he received. Caleb sat with glazed eyes, a broad smile, and a wistful look as he again allowed his mind to wander the paths of a possible future with his Clancy and it brought joy to his heart.

A journey borne of anticipation is longer for it. The night passed slowly for Caleb, tossing and turning with a mind that would not shut off to allow sleep to take over, he now rocked to the gentle sway of his appaloosa as he trailed behind Broken Shield. The smile that painted his face by the campfire remained and tugged even more at the corners of his mouth as his thoughts of Clancy and their future together filled his mind. Two Bits trotted alongside and occasionally looked up at Caleb and sensed the happiness that had captured the young man.

Scratch and the two mules followed behind Caleb

and the mountain man began to reminisce of days gone by and recalled their travels from Michigan territory. Those days were passed with the wilderness education of a young boy Scratch fondly called Squirt. Looking at the broad shouldered back of the man in front of him, Scratch started in again, "So Squirt, what kinda tree's that yonder?" as he pointed to a broad and towering tree shadowing the trail.

Caleb turned to look at his friend then back in the direction of his point and said, "Why, old man, that thar's a blue Spruce!"

"And that little flower next to it?"

"Ha! That's a columbine!"

"What about them tracks headin' up the slope thar?"

"Looks to me to be a couple mule deer, the big uns, probably a big buck!"

"Boy oh boy, ain'tchu a smart one! Sombuddy musta give you a good wilderness education! Wonder who that was?"

"Oh, some scraggly ole mountain man that thought he knew it all," replied Caleb as he turned in his saddle to grin at his friend.

It was midafternoon when the returning man hunters broke into the clearing that held the cabin. Three women sat side by side on the front step with knees drawn up, chins resting in their palms and elbows on their knees. Clancy and her bright red hair was framed by the two raven haired women of the wilderness but all three sported broad smiles and sparkling eyes. They remained seated as they watched the men and animals fill the clearing and Caleb quickly exhausted his patience.

Jumping from his mount he ran toward the women as Clancy stood up and ran to greet him. With arms spread wide she welcomed his embrace and kiss as they held on to each other in fear of being separated again. Another kiss and a tight hug, then Clancy pushed back from Caleb and stood with hands on her hips and a pout on her face and said, "And what do you mean by passing me by and letting me sit on that ledge for two days?"

"I didn't know you were there, honest!" he said with his face showing deep concern.

Clancy smiled and reached for another hug as she said, "I know you didn't but while I was waiting for you on that ledge I sure told you a thing or two!"

Arm in arm they walked toward the cabin as the other two women went to greet their men. Scratch busied himself with the animals and was heard talking to himself as he muttered, "Women! Can't live with 'em, and can't live without 'em. Guess I'm gonna have to get me another'n."

ALTHOUGH NO ONE SAID ANYTHING, EVERYONE knew. It was not a topic of conversation but the assumption among the people was nothing new. The older women nodded their heads in agreement as they had so often before as it seemed like this was destined by the Great Spirit and the people were happy.

Five women were gathered by a pile of recently tanned buffalo hides and were chattering among themselves as they pieced together the large hides to form a new lodge. The lodge of Black Kettle's woman was a beehive of activity with several women entering and leaving and the constant hum of woman talk continued unabated. Broken Shield, Leaf and Jeremiah were away on a visit to Leaf's people, the Crow that dwelt on the Eastern slopes of the Absaroka. Scratch and Talks to the Wind, or Caleb, were due to return from a buffalo hunt in the Wind River valley. It seemed like an ordinary day in the village but just a little busier than normal. After all, preparing for a wedding was a big event in the village.

In the busy lodge, Laughing Waters was the center of activity as she held some beadwork on her lap. A matching pair of circular design, the bold blue background highlighted the bright yellow sun with extending rays. From the bottom of the orbs hung long strings of multi-colored but matching beads in a fringe pattern accenting the design. These would be attached to the long braids of the redhead that would be adorned for this special day. Two other women were carefully cutting the long braids at the bottom of each arm of the dress. These braids would be almost two feet in length and would be decorated with beads in a matching pattern to the braid holders. With the bottom edge of the skirt in her lap, a third woman had begun the beadwork on the bottom fringe. Separating the two women working on the sleeve fringe, a grey headed matriarch worked on the delicate design of blue beads and porcupine quills across the bosom of the dress.

"So, Waters, tradition says there will be an exchange of gifts between the bride's family and the man's family, but since you and White Wolf are the same family, who gets the gifts?" asked Squash Blossom whose question elicited giggles from all the workers.

"I told Jeremiah he could just give me gifts and that would be good," she replied with a smile as she glanced at the quiet redhead busying herself behind the working women.

"Will you still have the feast for the elders to instruct the two the night before?"

"Yes, we have already spoken to the elders and the grandmothers that will be there." The women nodded their head in approval and continued their work and chatter as well as the usual jesting of the bride to be. The traditional wedding lodge was to be finished the next day and the feast would be held in that lodge. Before the wedding the lodge would be moved to a more isolated location deeper in the trees to provide the necessary privacy for the new couple. The day of the wedding, the village would have a feast and then the ceremony would follow. If all went well, the wedding would be in two days.

Before a man would be accepted as a possible husband among the people, he must first prove himself as a hunter and warrior that could provide for and protect a family. This was not often accomplished until the late 20's or even early 30's for most men but Caleb had already been proven and accepted as a capable hunter and warrior. Now returning to the village with Scratch, the two men each led a heavily laden mule with the meat and hides from two buffalo recently taken on their hunt. This was the third day of their hunting trip and Caleb was anxious to get back to Clancy and the coming ceremony. For the last two days, Scratch had been merciless in his banter and talk about women and marriage and how it's so much better to be 'footloose and fancy free.'

"Now, be honest Uncle Scratch, if you could find another woman that'd put up with you, wouldn't you tie the knot again?" asked Caleb.

"You mean to tell me after all I been tryin' ta' git through yore thick skull, you really think I'd get hitched again?" replied an exasperated scruff of a man.

"Yeah, I do! Course you'd have to find someone to put

up with you. I guess she'd have to be blind, deaf, and ugly to boot!" kidded Caleb as he grinned at his friend.

"Oh Pshaw, Squirt, I've had 'em lined up wantin' to marry up wit' me, but I just couldn't find it in me to break so many hearts and pick just one."

Caleb was thinking about Walking Dove, the widow of Jeremiah's adopted father, Ezekiel. She was much younger than Ezekiel and her twins by Ezekiel were now grown and just older than Caleb. The woman stood almost a head taller than Scratch, but Caleb had noticed the two of them keeping company and some of the people were thinking they would be a good match.

With Walking Dove having her own lodge and several horses and other gear, she was considered by many to be a wealthy woman and Scratch would be a good provider for them. Caleb and his Pa had talked about it before and both agreed they would like to see the couple together. The thought of Scratch being considered his grandfather brought a smile to his face and he looked at the man he called Uncle and tried to picture him as a mate to Walking Dove.

Arriving in the village, the two hunters were greeted by several women that would be in charge of the wedding feast and they walked alongside Caleb and patted him on his leg and smiled up at the man that would soon be a husband to Sun of the Morning. One woman spoke, "Talks to the Wind is a good provider, his lodge will always be warm and full of meat. You are a good man." Caleb smiled but thought, *I like the sound of that,' . . . a good man.'* Stopping his mount beside the lodge of the Shaman that now belonged to Waters, he dropped to the ground and taking the reins of Scratch's horse and his own, he walked them to a tether behind the lodge. The mules and meat had already been commandeered by the women and he would find the animals tethered beside his after the meat had been unloaded.

Scratching at the entrance, he asked if he could come in but the clatter of voices from within prevented his admittance and he soon heard Waters voice that instructed him to return to the cabin and tend to the animals there. She would be staying with Sun of the Morning here in the village and he could come back the next day. With a shrug of his shoulders, he looked for Scratch and saw just his back as it disappeared into the lodge of Walking Dove, so he mounted up and headed for the cabin.

Early the next morning he was rousted from his bedroll in the loft by his father. Jeremiah had returned well after dark and an exhausted Caleb had slept through his arrival and subsequent usual snoring the night through.

"Come on sleepy head, we got chores ta do. We need to get them animals to the upper meadow and then get on up to the village. For some reason they think you oughta be in on this shindig," chuckled his Pa.

A wide awake and anxious Caleb hastened about his business as he helped his Pa take the remaining horses and mules to the grassy meadow slightly uphill from their cabin. They had made a brush fence around the three-acre meadow and the animals always enjoyed the time of lazy grazing and unfettered wandering.

The sun had barely topped the trees when the two

men were well on their way to the village of the people. This would be the day for the feast with the elders and Caleb had wondered just what to expect but he had been kept in the dark and told he would learn what he needed to know when the time was right. *All this mystery, why can't they just tell a fella what to expect and make it easy on him?*

As they arrived, they saw the women erecting a new lodge at the edge of the village. This would be prepared for the feast with the elders and the family and would be ready in ample time. The two men were greeted by everyone they encountered with the women ducking their head and with hands over their mouths attempted to stifle the giggles and snickering. Each time this happened, Caleb would look at his Pa and shrug his shoulders in wonder.

Three days had passed since Caleb had last seen Clancy and as he entered the new lodge behind his Pa, he noticed her sitting beside Waters. Clad in a typical buckskin tunic with simple designs across the chest and fringe hanging from the arms, she sat with legs crossed that revealed the fringed leggings she wore under the tunic. What held his attention was the long red braids that fell down her shoulders. He didn't remember ever seeing her in braids and the effect of the pulled back hair that showed the glow of her freckled skin and the radiance of her smile captured his attention and stirred his spirit with affection. *Wow, she's beautiful!* he thought. He seated himself beside his father and the two were now separated by both Jeremiah and Waters. Two women served the group beginning with the elders, the grandmothers (older respected women that served as elders for the women), the parents and finally the couple to be joined. Little conversation occurred during the meal and as soon as the meal was finished, Broken Shield, the leader of the village began.

"This is a time of instruction, a time for those that have climbed the four hills of life and gained much wisdom to share with you. Each one will speak as they believe the Great Spirit leads, or as you would say, as your God would lead. Listen well and heed the wisdom and you will have many years of happiness."

The oldest of the men began and offered his bit of advice concerning the responsibility of the man to always provide for his lodge. Another spoke about the need for loving his woman and his children and still another told of the need for bravery in protecting his people. And so it went for almost an hour as each one of the elders and grandmothers offered their bits of wisdom and counsel. As they finished, Broken Shield began to recite an old wedding prayer as he said, "Be:he:teiht, our Great Creator speaks to us . . .

Above you are the stars, below you are the stones. As time does pass, remember, like a star should your love be constant and like a stone should your love be firm.

Be close, yet not too close, possess one another, yet be understanding. Have patience with the other; for storms will come, but they will go quickly.

Be free in giving of affection and warmth, make love often and be sensuous to one another. Have no fear and let not the ways or words of the unenlightened give you unease.

For the Great Spirit is with you, now and always.

The time together concluded with the giving of gifts to all the elders and grandmothers. The gifts were nothing elaborate, just common trade goods, but the tradition was kept and all departed happy. Tomorrow would be the big day.

The day seemed to begin with the wedding feast although the preparations were not complete until mid-day. Everyone was in a celebratory mood and the feast was soon complete and the drums began and the dancing shortly followed. After two hours of feasting and dancing, the drums stopped and people started to gather near the lodge of the Shaman. Without any instruction given, the people formed two parallel lines through the village that ended before the lodge. This was to be the path of the couple to be joined.

Caleb was with Jeremiah, Shield and Scratch in the lodge of Broken Shield and the men instructed Caleb as he donned his specially prepared attire. He did not know his mother had made this special tunic and leggings for him and he was amazed at the simplistic beauty and soft-ness of the white tanned doeskin. A simple band of blue beads and porcupine quills stretched across the chest of the tunic and long fringe fell from the sleeves. Fringe decorated the sides of the leggings and the simple bead-work on the moccasins matched that of the tunic.

At the direction of the men, he stepped from the lodge and made his way to the other lodge for his Sun of the Morning. He scratched at the entrance, and the flap was thrown back and the woman emerged to the gasp of her husband to be. The beautiful garment of white doeskin matched his, but held more decorative bead work and designs. As she stood erect, her shy smile topped off the most beautiful sight he thought he had ever seen.

He stood speechless and immobile for several moments as he just took in the image of his beloved. As his smile spread, he reached for her hand and they started down the gauntlet of well- wishers toward the Shaman's lodge. While they walked, they recited to one another the pledges of the seven steps for happiness that had been memorized before. With each pledge of faith, love and loyalty, their commitment to one another grew stronger with the expressions of fidelity.

Arriving at the shaman's lodge, Laughing Waters emerged to stand beside Broken Shield. Jeremiah stood to the side and watched with a proud father's eyes. Shield spoke first, "You have come to be joined together?"

Talks to the Wind responded, "Yes my chief. We ask your blessing for our lodge."

Laughing Waters spoke, "You have taken the path of your lives to this place. You have walked the trail of the seven steps and have vowed your love and faith to each other, have you not?"

Sun of the Morning said, "Yes, Shaman, we have vowed to one another."

Waters reached for their hands and placing one on top of the other and holding them both in hers, she said, "As you have vowed together and before God, you are now husband and wife."

At that proclamation, a collective 'Whooop' and

cheers rose from the crowd and laughter broke out among them all. Taking Clancy in his arms, Caleb embraced his wife, then joining hands they turned to go to their lodge.

Jeremiah touched Caleb on his shoulder and said, "You two come back here," and led the way behind the lodge. Tethered there were the big appaloosa of Caleb's and beside him stood a new mare for Clancy. Both animals were adorned with matching blankets spread over the saddles but there was enough exposed that it was easy to see the new mare was a perfect match for the appaloosa of Caleb. Both animals had white spotted rumps, dark chests and belly, blaze faces and black stockings. Jeremiah said, "These two should produce some pretty nice colts for you to start your herd with, don't ya think?"

Clancy jumped to put her arms around Jeremiah's neck and said, "Thanks Pa, she's a beaut!"

"Well, you two better get on outta here, your lodge has been set up down that trail yonder, just over by the lake. We don't expect to see you for a day or so, but you know where we are." With Waters standing beside him, Jeremiah extended a hand to wave to the newlyweds as they trotted down the trail, side by side and hand in hand.

THE END

*A LOOK AT TO THE MEDICINE BOW,
THE NEXT BOOK IN THE BUCKSKIN
CHRONICLES*

Sometimes in life, the shortest distance between where you are and where you want to be is not necessarily the best route. Life often takes you on a much longer trail before you reach the goal you were destined for, and this circuitous route usually has valuable life lessons. These are the lessons that littered the path of the lives of Clancy and Caleb as they fled from the sorrow of the mountains and searched for answers in all the wrong places. Thinking the big city would provide refuge and salve for painful memories, they learned where ever they went there were new lessons to learn and memories to be made. With both having a love for the mountains and the often solitary lifestyle, the pull of the city would not readily release its grip but they would have to chart their own course.

With an opportunity provided by new found friendships and the possibility of a new direction for their lives, they seek to return to the mountains to find their own nirvana and a new beginning to establish their home and their legacy. The shining mountains and green valley of the Medicine Bow range that nestles in the Southern most part of Wyoming territory beckons them and the promise of a new life gives hope where there was none. Now is when they find out if they have the strength and stamina to build a new life in the mountains of the Medicine Bow.

AVAILABLE NOW FROM B.N. RUNDELL AND WOLFPACK PUBLISHING

Born and raised in Colorado into a family of ranchers and cowboys, B.N. is the youngest of seven sons. Juggling bull riding, skiing, and high school, graduation was a launching pad for a hitch in the Army Paratroopers. After the army, he finished his college education in Springfield, MO, and together with his wife and growing family, entered the ministry as a Baptist preacher.

Together, B.N. and Dawn raised four girls that are now married and have made them proud grandparents. With many years as a successful pastor and educator, he retired from the ministry and followed in the footsteps of his entrepreneurial father and started a successful insurance agency, which is now in the hands of his trusted nephew. He has also been a successful audiobook narrator and has recorded many books for several award-winning authors. Now finally realizing his life-long dream, B.N. has turned his efforts to writing a variety of books, from children's picture books and young adult adventure books, to the historical fiction and western genres which are his first love.